DOGGONE!

The small dog continued to growl. Didi looked past him and saw what seemed to be a wildflower growing right out of the sandy soil. Her assistant Trent saw it also. He broke a limb off a stunted oak, sprinted past the dog, and began to scrape away at the sandy earth. As he did so, the wildflower emerged in its full shape: it was a lock of hair. The ground was so porous and the grave so shallow, it took only moments to realize what was being excavated—three partially decomposed bodies: Rose Vigdor and her two German shepherds.

Don't Miss the Other Titles in this Series:

Dr. Nightingale
Follows a
Canine Clue

A DEIRDRE QUINN
NIGHTINGALE MYSTERY

Lydia Adamson

A SIGNET BOOK

SIGNET
Published by New American Library, a division of
Penguin Putnam Inc., 375 Hudson Street,
New York, New York 10014, U.S.A.
Penguin Books Ltd, 27 Wrights Lane,
London W8 5TZ, England
Penguin Books Australia Ltd,
Ringwood, Victoria, Australia
Penguin Books Canada Ltd, 10 Alcorn Avenue,
Toronto, Ontario, Canada M4V 3B2
Penguin Books (N.Z.) Ltd, 182–190 Wairau Road,
Auckland 10, New Zealand

Penguin Books Ltd, Registered Offices:
Harmondsworth, Middlesex, England

First published by Signet, an imprint of New American Library,
a division of Penguin Putnam Inc.

First Printing, July 2001
10 9 8 7 6 5 4 3 2 1

PUBLISHER'S NOTE
This is a work of fiction. Names, characters, places, and incidents either
are the product of the author's imagination or are used fictitiously, and
any resemblance to actual persons, living or dead, events, or locales is
entirely coincidental.

Chapter 1

As she trudged through the thick, sweet-smelling ground cover toward the herd of grazing bovines, Didi for some reason thought of an old piece of nonsense verse:

> There once was a cow named Priscilla
> Her milk came out sarsparilla
> She waited for dark
> And then started to bark
> And that's why we hired a gorilla

What a stupid ditty, she thought, but to be among cows always made her childish. Particularly in a field in late summer. Sweet black and white beasts dotting the green green grass. It was like living in a beautiful watercolor painting. Didi winced at her misplaced romanticism. She was, after all, Dr. Deirdre Quinn Nightingale, DVM, a working vet going to visit a sick cow, not a whimsical travel writer. *And* she was a working vet whose practice and income were shrinking. Every client was a treasure.

Walking beside her was a gawky middle-aged woman named Lee Ayers. This was her cow farm and it was called precisely that—The Cow Farm. It was Didi's first visit to the farm and first meeting with Lee, but she had heard of Mrs. Ayers and her operation. Lee Ayers was one of several people who had started up small "organic" dairy farms amid the ruins of the commercial dairy industry in Dutchess County.

They were nothing like their failed predecessors. They had very small herds. They fed the cows no commercial feed. They avoided all antibiotics. They milked in a primitive fashion, with old-fashioned pails. They delivered the milk themselves to a small cooperative processing plant. They put the milk in bottles, not cartons. They didn't sell the milk in supermarkets, only in posh suburban and big city gourmet shops. They rode the nostalgia wave like surfers.

Dr. Nightingale had made no judgment on them one way or the other. Cows were cows, and the more the merrier. In one area, in fact, the new dairy people had gained her respect. They knew how to plant and rotate fodder and grazing crops—clover, alfalfa, rye. Their cows ate well.

Charlie Gravis, Didi's geriatric veterinary assistant, was walking behind the two women, wheezing and cursing under his breath, the "rounds" bag under his right arm.

Didi smiled at his behavior. The morning was already warm, but it wasn't the summer heat that was making him irascible. The old dairy farmer hated anything to do with the word *organic.* It literally drove him into an unreasoning fury.

Suddenly they were right in among the cows.

"Look there, doc!" Lee said in an urgent whisper, pointing to a large cow grazing calmly not ten feet from them.

"That's Betty," she noted.

Betty was a bit swaybacked and had a very long, swishing tail.

"Now watch," Lee Ayers said.

She called out in a loud voice: "Get on, Betty!"

The cow tensed and jerked her head up. Her eyes showed terror. She urinated. Then she began to walk in a bizarre, stiff-legged gait, like a crippled toy soldier. Then she stopped, urinated again, and finally went back to grazing peacefully.

"Well?" Lee Ayers demanded.

Didi didn't respond. She had never seen anything quite like it.

"Watch this," Lee said. She picked up a small pebble and flung it lightly at Betty. It hit the animal's flank.

Once again the cow went through her strange ritual, repeating the steps in exactly the same order.

"Look," Didi said, "let's get Betty into the barn and I'll examine her. We'll also start a workup—blood, urine, stool."

Lee Ayers produced a lead rope, and she and the doctor started walking slowly toward Betty.

"Hold up!" Charlie called out suddenly. He hadn't moved at all.

Didi turned to him impatiently. "What?"

"It's the Grass Staggers, Doc."

Didi was startled by the sureness of his diagnosis.

"No, Charlie. That's a beef cattle thing."

"Dairy cows get it too! I seen it before! At least twice, in the late seventies."

Lee Ayers jumped in: "What is he talking about?"

Didi elucidated. "Grass Staggers is a farmers' name for hypomagnesemic tetany. It's a metabolic disorder. The low levels of magnesium and high levels of potassium in certain grazing pastures combine to limit magnesium absorption. In other words, we're talking about a major deficiency."

Didi paused. The wisdom of Charlie's diagnosis became apparent. These "organic" cows ingested only pasture—no commercial feed whatsoever.

"Is it bad?"

"From what I know of the disorder, Mrs. Ayers, Betty is in no danger . . . *now*. But the later stages get nasty. Convulsions and death."

"Can't you do anything?"

"Oh yes. It's treated quickly and easily. An IV injection of calcium and magnesium, along with a sedative."

"Maybe you ought to do the whole herd," Lee suggested.

"Yes," Didi agreed. "I think that . . ."

Her cell phone began to ring like a chirping bird. Didi pulled the phone out of the side pocket of her carpenter's jeans and answered the call.

It was Trent Tucker, one of her "elves." Like Charlie Gravis, Mrs. Tunney, and Abigail, Trent had come with the house and property that Didi inherited from her mother. The daughter could not in good conscience kick out the mother's charity cases, so they remained, working for room and board. Trent was essentially the handyman, a diffident, difficult kid of twenty-four who could never find real work.

"I'm calling from the old quarry," he said.

"What are you doing up there?"

"Look, this sounds crazy, but I just saw Huck."

"You mean Rose's Huck?" Didi asked incredulously.

"Yeah. The Corgi. He just trotted out of the woods, skinny and all beat up. Saw me and ran back in."

She didn't know what to say. When her best friend in Hillsbrook, Rose Vigdor, had suddenly packed up and left six months ago without telling anyone or leaving a forwarding address, she had taken her three dogs with her, of course. The two German shepherds, Aretha and Bozo, and the Corgi, Huck. No one had seen hide nor hair of Rose and her entourage since then. No one had heard from her.

"Did you hear what I said?" Trent asked.

"I heard."

Dr. Nightingale tried to think clearly. What were the possibilities? Only two. Trent had just seen a stray Corgi. Since it wasn't a common breed in the Hillsbrook area, he assumed it was Huck. Or Rose was visiting the area secretly. But why? Why wouldn't she look Didi up? Why wouldn't she explain why she had left so suddenly and without a word?

Didi turned to Lee Ayers: "I'll be back late this afternoon with the IV preparations. About four o'clock. Just have them all in the barn by three."

Dr. Nightingale and her assistant climbed into the red Jeep and drove five miles to the old stone quarry that had for many years functioned as the town dump. It was closed down in the mid-eighties and filled in with gravel. The quarry was located in the Ridge, the ugliest and poorest section of Hillsbrook, a series of small hills dotted with cabins and derelict trailers. It was rural poverty at its worst; no electricity, no phones, no plumbing. The main industry of the Ridge was stolen car and truck parts.

Trent Tucker was waiting for them, standing alongside his battered pickup truck on the dirt road that led to the quarry. It was the road that the dump trucks used to use—sloping precipitously toward the cusp of the quarry.

"He came out of the woods over there. Then he saw me and ran back in."

"Okay. Let's spread out and cover the area," Didi said.

They distanced themselves about twenty feet from each other and entered the woods. It was difficult going, wading through the thick low-lying shrubs and the stunted pin oak and jack pines. The air was dense. Mosquitoes hovered in clusters, wood beetles scrambled over their feet, and horseflies buzzed about their ears.

"Here, Huck! Here, Huck!" they kept calling.

They had penetrated about a hundred yards from the road when they heard the growl—a low, spitting, ugly sound.

Then they saw him. *Oh yes*, Didi thought, *that is surely Huck.*

The dog was sitting on his haunches, snarling. The clearing in which he sat was sandy.

"He's so damn mangy he looks like a squirrel," Charlie noted. They stopped about ten feet from him. Didi crouched down and held out her hand.

"Here, boy. Come over here. Come on."

The small dog kept his place and continued to growl.

Then Didi looked past him and saw what seemed to be a wild flower growing right out of the sandy soil. Trent saw it also. He broke a limb off a stunted oak, sprinted past the dog, and began to scrape away at the sandy earth.

Huck charged him and fastened his teeth on Trent's boot. Trent ignored the dog.

As he scraped, the wild flower emerged in its

full shape. One didn't need a field manual to identify it. It was a lock of hair.

The ground was so porous and the grave so shallow, it took only moments to realize what was being excavated—three partially decomposed bodies: Rose Vigdor and the two German shepherds.

Only the silver dog tags and the blond hair had maintained their form and color.

The little dog grew weak in his assault on Trent's boot. He lay down and stared at Dr. Nightingale. She could not meet his gaze.

Chapter 2

It was not the usual breakfast at the Nightingale house. For one, Dr. Nightingale was seated with her elves at the kitchen table—something she rarely did because she felt awkward trying to be an equal while she was in effect the boss. They were her indentured servants, like it or not.

And there were visitors in the kitchen—also a rarity. The Hillsbrook plainclothes detective (the only one in town), Albert Voegler, and a state trooper homicide detective (in civilian clothes), Lewis Mikoyan.

To make matters even stranger, Mrs. Tunney was too upset to make oatmeal, something which she did every morning, no matter the season or the lack of enthusiasm for said dish on the part of the other elves.

Finally, and strangest of all, Mrs. Tunney had so far this morning kept her mouth shut. She hadn't harangued anyone. She had not complained. She had not even hummed.

In fact, she was quite depressed.

The death of Rose Vigdor was dreadful, even though Mrs. Tunney had expected some tragedy with that young lady. After all, Rose Vigdor never ate a good meal—just brown rice and those ridiculous health food chips.

The visit by these two police officers made Mrs. Tunney even more uncomfortable, depressed, and confused.

Mrs. Tunney truly disliked Allie Voegler. She had tried subtly to persuade Miss Quinn (she always called Didi by her mother's maiden name) to break off her engagement to him. She had been very happy when they did break up. Now, she knew, they were lovers again. As for the state homicide detective—she detested bald men with moustaches.

Mrs. Tunney kept looking from time to time at Didi . . . brief, furtive glances filled with compassion . . . poor girl . . . all of this was no good.

Abigail, seated to the right of Didi and to the left of Charlie Gravis, was the only one who seemed happy. She was beating a spoon lightly against her coffee cup. But Abigail was always strange and hard to fathom—tall, thin, golden haired, a beautiful singing voice . . . with a brain that was always one synapse short of resolution.

Mikoyan, the state trooper homicide detective, wearing a pressed white short-sleeve shirt and a pair of baggy gray pants, sat down heavily on a small kitchen ladder and said, looking straight at Dr. Nightingale: "We have some preliminary data. They were all killed by a blunt instrument. Probably a shovel. Brought with great force against the skull. They had been dead and buried about a month."

Dr. Nightingale did not say a word in response. Nor did anyone else. Allie Voegler kept his eyes on the floor. He seemed discomforted. He began to sway slightly, his large frame tense.

"Voegler here tells me," Mikoyan continued, "that you were her friend."

"Yes, I was," Didi replied emphatically.

"Can you give me some next of kin to contact?"

"No."

Mikoyan arched his eyebrows. "But you just said—"

"Yes. I said she was my friend. My best friend. But she was very secretive about some things."

"And she left the Hillsbrook area how long ago?" Mikoyan pressed on.

"Maybe six months ago."

"And you never filed a missing person report?"

"No. It never occurred to me. Rose was mercurial. She just packed up and left with the dogs. I thought she'd be back in a few days. Then I thought—well, I don't really know what I thought as the time passed. But I never believed she was in any kind of trouble. Rose could take care of herself."

"Obviously, Dr. Nightingale, you were wrong about that."

Mrs. Tunney had a sudden desire to fling the sugar bowl at this Mikoyan. Charlie Gravis spotted the danger and waggled his finger at her. She glared back at him.

Mikoyan asked, "What were you doing just prior to your discovery of the body, doctor?"

"I was about to treat some cows for magnesium deficiency."

"And then the call came in?"

"Yes."

"That your boy saw one of the dogs. One of Rose Vigdor's dogs?"

"Yes. Her Corgi. But he's not my boy."

"I didn't mean he was your son. You don't seem much older than he is, Dr. Nightingale."

"He lives and works here," Didi said.

Then, for the first time during this conversation or interrogation, she looked at Albert Voegler. And he looked at her, a bit shamefaced, as if he did not like the way the state trooper was proceeding but he had no say in the matter.

"I'll be in touch," Mikoyan said.

The two visitors let themselves out of the kitchen door. The moment they were outside, Mrs. Tunney said to Didi: "I'll make you some eggs, dearie."

Dr. Nightingale shook her head. She wasn't hungry. She never ate breakfast.

Then she did something unusual. She reached across the wooden table and took Mrs. Tunney's hand. The gesture was so sudden and so unprecedented that the older woman seemed to lapse into a state of shock.

Charlie Gravis and Ike Badian sat in the latter's decrepit pickup truck, across the road from Rose Vigdor's property, on which was located the huge old barn that Rose had lived in like a squatter, and which she had been continually renovating.

Charlie and Ike had been estranged for several months because of Charlie's most recent attempt to make some money, in which he had embroiled Ike in a restaurant scheme in Ike's barn. It had ended in disaster when the two old dairy farmers had served a woodchuck dish (not identified as such) which they'd been told was authentic nineteenth-century Hudson Valley cuisine. On the restaurant's opening night, alas, some customers had stumbled upon the woodchucks being prepared in the bathtub—and that was that. Even the Board of Health had investigated.

But now the wounds were healed. Charlie had told Ike what the state trooper said; they had had a few beers in town and cursed Burt Conyers, the mad poet-laureate who had convinced them to serve the woodchuck dish; then they had driven out to Rose's place for no particular reason except they had to go somewhere.

"You know," Charlie noted, "the summer is almost over and we haven't had a real hot day yet."

"How hot do you want it? I mean, it got up to ninety-seven yesterday."

"I want to see the roads crack and the grass shrivel in the shade."

Badian chewed his stumpy cigar and pondered his friend's sudden poetic turn.

When he was finished pondering and chewing, he asked: "How come you're not working today?"

"The doc is out of sorts. It kinda makes sense.

She really liked the Rose girl. Anyway, she'd go out on emergencies if necessary."

"There's not much cow work for a vet around here anymore," Ike said.

"That's for sure. But there's a vet in Delaware County who wants her to go into partnership with him."

"She considering it?"

"Don't know. She don't talk her mind to me much."

"Did she pick up any of those new thorough-bred stables?"

"No," Charlie replied, and then pointed at the looming barn across the road. "It sure is a beauty."

Ike asked: "Anyone been paying taxes on it?"

"Don't know. Like the state trooper said—they are trying to find relatives of hers. Or someone."

There was another long silence. Crows were circling the barn.

"A shovel, right?" asked Ike.

"Yeah. A shovel it was. To the back of the head. Had to be some kind of sick bastard to do that . . . to the dogs also."

"Except the little one."

"Yeah. The Corgi. He got away."

"Where's he now?"

"Abigail's taking care of him. But she's keeping him away from the yard dogs for a while. He's staying in Doc's horse barn. You remember it? One side for her horse. In the other side I keep my pigs."

"I thought you ate all the pigs."

"Not funny, Ike. But I'll tell you something that is funny. I had a dream about cows."

"So?"

"I don't remember if it was last night or the night before," Charlie said. "But in the dream I was hired to set up a money-making dairy farm operation in some distant land. They sent me a first class air travel ticket. Anyway, when I arrived, the place was full of ice and snow. The people lived in ice houses, sort of like igloos. But what was really crazy was, the cows were grazing on the ice and snow. And they looked real fat and happy."

"That's a helluva dream, Charlie."

"Yeah. But it gets stranger. And it's no longer funny. Because when I go out to the snow pasture to check out the herd, I see they ain't pulling grass from underneath the snow and ice—they're pulling little fish and gobbling them up. Can you imagine cows eating fish? Anyway, in the dream I keep walking around staring at those fool cows and I'm getting more and more afraid. You know why? Because I know they're gonna pull up a real big fish sooner or later. I mean a big ugly dangerous fish."

"You mean a shark?"

"Maybe. Anyway, then I woke up."

"What do you think it means, Charlie?"

"Trouble."

Ike Badian burst out laughing. Then he said: "Look, Charlie, given our age and the state of our finances—and given that we ain't got no future at all in any way, shape, or form, much less cows—even trouble is welcome. Right?"

Charlie nodded his assent.

It was four-thirty in the afternoon. Albert Voegler sat on the edge of the bed, naked except for a bath towel over his lap. He was a large man, still muscular but adding weight each year, rounding out his angles. His hair was thick and wild. The newly grown beard seemed, paradoxically, to soften his face. He looked, Didi thought, like a monkish bear.

Didi stood there, fully clothed, ten feet from the bed.

For the past month or so, since they had reconciled, the scenario had been the same. She arrived late in the afternoon. They made love. She went home.

Both had seemed to want it that way. Perhaps

to avoid trouble. They had a mercurial past together. Breakups. Engagements. Breakups. Friendship. Enmity. It had been a roller coaster. And now this—calm repetitive sex that was totally predictable.

Didi hadn't minded it at all. Until today. The pall of sadness was crushing her.

"You didn't have to come today," he said. "I would have understood."

She walked to the bed and sat down beside him. From where they sat they could see through the window to the Hillsbrook Library building across the street. Allie's apartment was on the second floor in a farm house, right smack in the middle of the village.

She leaned back. "I keep thinking," she said, "how stupid I was. How was it possible that I didn't think anything was wrong? My best friend packs up and leaves without a word and all I think is, well, that's Rose . . . she'll be back soon."

Allie didn't respond.

She stared at his profile.

"Month after month and she doesn't return or contact me," Dr. Nightingale continued, "and I do nothing, think nothing is wrong."

Again, he was silent. She wanted him to say something, to console her. But, she realized, he was never consoling. This latest permutation of their relationship was about sex, and sure, intimacy—but it was not geared to bad times. Personally, that is. She was a vet and he a police officer, so bad times in the world was endemic—violence, disease, death.

This lack of an abiding consolation was probably why she did not truly love him . . . at least, not in the way he loved her. She never made declarations of love. He made them all the time, and when he was drinking, he made them so loudly it embarrassed her.

She stood up suddenly and cried out: "I cannot bear thinking of that grave! Of her hair sticking out of the gravel and mud like an old mop!"

He stood. He took her hands.

"Let me make you some coffee," he said quietly, formally.

She realized that something was peculiar. He had offered coffee in his police manner and had put on his cop face. Did he know something? Had something even more gruesome been discovered? Had the trooper and he uncovered . . . what? Oh, she knew that cop face.

He walked into the small kitchen and began to boil water for instant coffee. The towel had dropped away from his body. He was naked.

"I don't want any coffee," she called to him.

He ignored her and kept tinkering with the kettle.

"Did you hear me, Allie?"

He didn't answer.

"You have to tell me everything you know."

He turned and stared at her across the space that separated them. "About what?" he asked angrily.

"About Rose."

"I don't think you want to know," he replied.

"Are you crazy?" she shot back, furious.

"Okay. Sure. Why not. Let me tell you something you don't know. Do you remember where you were just before she vanished?"

"Yes. I had gone to Atlantic City for a veterinary convention. And then some bad things happened there and I had to stay on."

He nodded, but kept silent.

"So?" she pressed.

"Well," he said slowly, "I was worried about you. You were floating around. I didn't know where you were. I went to see Rose."

"So?"

"It was strange. We were talking. We started to argue. And then, I don't know what happened."

"You're not making sense, Allie."

"We made love."

"What?"

"Rose and I. We made love. On the floor of the barn."

He couldn't look at her now. He looked past her.

All the strength drained from Didi's legs. She sat down again on the bed.

He put on a pair of pants, talking to her as he did so. She didn't hear a word he said. She stared at the distant kettle on the stove. If she had a weapon, she thought, she would use it on him. She would kill him. She walked out, unsteadily.

Chapter 3

Seated on the naked ground in lotus position at six o'clock in the morning, Dr. Nightingale tried mightily to perform her usual yogic breathing exercises with energy and precision.

After about ten minutes she realized it was no use—the depression, the lack of sleep, and the inability to hold down her food had triumphed.

She walked into the kitchen, greeted the elves at the breakfast table, took a cup of coffee, walked outside again, and headed toward the barn.

Everything, she realized, was now happening to her in slow motion. That was why the barn seemed so far away. All the buildings and objects seemed to be receding, but what was really happening was that her senses were impaired.

When she walked inside the barn she was already drenched with sweat.

The moment she entered, her horse, Promise

Me, started a ruckus, hoping no doubt for a carrot, an apple, or delight of all delights, several chunks of brown sugar that Dr. Nightingale shamefacedly cadged from a new hip coffee shop in the village.

Didi ignored him, and the pigs, who had also started up in response to the horse.

She walked to the stall that had been set up and screened in as Huck's temporary home. The Corgi seemed to be relaxed. There was plenty of food and water. The perimeter was secure. And Abigail had provided a few rawhide dog bones.

Didi stared at the small, stumpy dog. Huck knew everything. He had been with Rose every step of the way. He had seen and escaped the butchery. He was the living witness. But neither she nor the authorities spoke Corgi tongue. It was a very exotic language.

She started to ease herself onto the barn floor to spend some time with Huck when she heard someone calling. She walked to the open barn door and peered out.

Yes, Mrs. Tunney was yelling something and pointing.

Her eyes followed and saw that a vehicle had pulled up by the side of the house. The yard dogs were leaping and yelping all around it.

Didi waved to Mrs. Tunney and headed toward the vehicle. Usually when cars pulled up at this hour of the morning it was a motorist with a wounded cat or dog or deer he had run over. She had become in a sense Dr. Nightingale of the road-kill set.

Halfway to the vehicle she realized it was Allie Voegler's car. She stopped dead in her tracks. She didn't want to see him or speak to him.

But then she realized he was not alone. Was that the state trooper in the car? What was his name? Mikoyan?

She moved a little closer. He stepped out of the car. She approached.

"Sorry to come by so early," he apologized, "but I have some information."

Didi kept her gaze away from Voegler. "I've been up a long time," she said.

"First of all, we've located a relation of Rose Vigdor. An aunt in Washington, D.C."

"That's good."

"She'll take the body. And the autopsy is complete. There is nothing new to report on that front. Trauma to the head. The blow was so severe she died instantly. And the dogs."

Didi smiled grimly.

"What's so funny?" Mikoyan asked.

"Nothing really. I just had the strange feeling

that you tell all friends of victims who are murdered that way the same story."

"Why would I do that?"

"So I would believe she was not buried alive."

"I'm just relaying to you information I received from the medical examiner's office."

"Okay."

"I also need some information from you."

"What?"

"Does the name Sonya Loomis ring a bell?"

"No."

"Are you sure? Think for a minute."

"I don't know anybody by that name."

"Then you weren't aware that Rose Vigdor used that name on occasion?"

"No. And I don't believe it."

"About three months ago a woman named Sonya Loomis began attending one of those Zen Buddhist retreats on the Hudson River. A place called Sunyata House, in Albertsville. After being in residence there for several weeks, she torched the place. There is a warrant for her arrest on arson and attempted homicide charges. We have a fingerprint match between Loomis and Vigdor."

The statement was so bizarre that Didi could not respond at all. She looked at Allie. He returned the look calmly, drumming his fingers on the steering wheel.

The yard dogs were now jumping up on Didi, moaning and whining and trying to kiss her face.

Mikoyan said: "Those are the healthiest yard dogs I've ever seen. But why shouldn't they be? You're a vet, aren't you, Dr. Nightingale?"

She didn't reply.

Mikoyan climbed back into the car. "If you recall anything about Sonya Loomis," he called out through the rolled-down window, "it would be helpful."

They drove off.

Charlie Gravis grimaced as he sipped the coffee in Ike Badian's cavernous ancient kitchen.

"How long your wife been dead?" he asked.

"A long time," Ike replied.

"What I can't figure out is why a man like you, who can wire a whole barn and dismantle a milking system and put it back together again, can't learn how to make a simple cup of coffee."

"You don't like it, go to the diner. Besides, don't you people ever have any work?"

"I don't know where the doc was yesterday afternoon, but when she came back she looked like a zombie. And this morning she seemed to be sleepwalking. Anyway, to make matters worse, about six-thirty in the morning up pops that state trooper homicide guy again. After he leaves, she goes to her room and stays there. About eight, I get an emergency call from Calvert."

"Who's he?"

"You remember him. That rich guy with the goats. Moved up here about five years ago. Anyway, he tells me three of his goats got some kind of infection in their eyes. And they're stumbling a lot. So I get up to Doc's room and tell her. She tells me to give the call to Randazzo."

"Who's Randazzo?"

"The vet Doc uses to cover for her when she goes on one of her trips. Anyway, why am I telling you this?"

"Because I asked why you and the doc aren't out on rounds."

"Well, I got other problems beside Doc's breakdown and your lousy coffee."

"Like what?"

"Like that damn dream. I had it again in blazing technicolor. Last night. And I woke up like a kid. I mean, Ike, it was embarrassing. I had pissed in my bed."

"It happens at our age."

"No. It was the dream. I was scared."

"Okay, Charlie, look. If it's bothering you that much, why don't you get it interpreted?"

"You mean go to a shrink?"

"No. You don't have the money for that. I mean, one of those dream ladies, like Stan Black's widow, Lily. Yeah, Lily Black."

"How much does she charge?"

"I don't know. Maybe ten bucks."

"Where does she live?"

"Where they always lived. She sold the farm but kept half an acre or so on the north edge and a small house."

"You take me there, Ike?"

"Sure. After coffee."

An hour later they pulled up to the low clapboard shack that looked like it had once been a hen house. Exiting the vehicle, they were immediately attacked by two tiny snarling terriers. Lily Black called them off and stood regarding her visitors from the front step, which seemed to be constructed from an orange crate.

"Damn," Charlie whispered to his friend, "she's an old woman now."

"No older than you, Charlie."

The woman's face brightened when she recognized them. She was wearing a housecoat with a red flower print and her white hair was pulled up in a bun. She squinted heavily. She was very thin, a bit stooped, and her bright yellow, almost gleeful slippers seemed five sizes too big for her.

"It's so nice to have a visit from Stan's friends," she said as she led them into the dwelling and made them sit on a day bed with rusty feet, guarded by the dogs, while she brought them milk and cookies.

The walls of the room were hung with old banners and prizes from innumerable county fairs. There were only two windows in the shack and the heat was stifling. The windows seemed to be nailed shut.

Once seated on a chair across from them, Lily Black seemed to act as if she had received a visit from mischievous schoolboys.

Charlie got right to the point.

"I want you to tell me about a dream I had. Ike says you charge ten dollars."

"That would be fair," she replied, gesturing with her hands that they should eat the repast she had provided.

Charlie dug two fives out of his pocket and slid them under the cookie plate. Then he started to recount the dream.

"Wait!" she interrupted. She walked over, stood very close to him, and took his hands in hers—kneading his knuckles hard for a moment. Then she held them lightly.

"Tell me," she said.

Charlie told her the recurring dream. How he was hired to set up a dairy operation in a strange land. How when he arrived he saw the people living in igloos and fat, happy, healthy cows grazing on snow and ice and pulling up and eating tiny fish. How he was confused by the fact that these cows ate fish. How he became fearful that they were going to pull up something horrible.

When he was finished, Lily released his hands and returned to her chair. She seemed to be mulling the situation over carefully.

Charlie became impatient. "Well?"

"You have had a predictive dream."

"Huh?"

"It foretells the future. What I glean from it is twofold. First, a violent demise. Then a fond remembrance."

"You mean I'm going to die a violent death? When? How?"

"That is all I will say."

Charlie glared at Ike, who shrugged. They walked out of the house and headed for the pickup.

Just as they were climbing in, the old lady burst out of the house, yelling: "Hold on!" She was waving something white in her hand.

When she reached them, she handed Charlie an envelope with a stamp on it.

She explained: "I forgot you live at the Nightingale house, Charlie. Here, give it to her so I don't have to mail it."

Charlie took the envelope and stared at it. Yes, it was addressed to Deirdre Quinn Nightingale, DVM.

"Who's it from?" Charlie asked, because there was no return address.

"A young woman named Rose. She came to see me about two months ago. She paid me to hold it for her. If I heard that anything bad had happened to her, I was to mail it. So I heard what happened to her and her dogs. So I am doing the right thing. And such a pretty girl she was."

Charlie and Ike drove off.

"That is weird, Charlie," Ike noted, meaning the letter.

But Charlie wasn't listening. What the hell had Lily Black meant? A violent demise and a fond remembrance? Was he really going to die in a conflagration? Today? Tomorrow? Now? And who in hell would remember him fondly? Ike?

Albert Voegler was the only customer at the bar in the Route 44 Café. It was eleven minutes past midnight when he walked in and ordered a nonalcoholic beer.

It had been probably the worst forty-eight hours in his life.

His confession to Didi about that one-night stand with Rose Vigdor was without parallel for stupidity. What was the point of it? Why had he done it?

As for that state trooper homicide detective, Mikoyan, being assigned immediately to the Vigdor murder—that was degrading in the extreme. It was Voegler's jurisdiction. He was experienced. He had known the victim. But of course he knew why Mikoyan had been assigned. Allie was back on the Hillsbrook police force after two months of suspension during which he was forced to seek psychiatric help for his behavioral problems. The event precipitating his suspension had been the manhandling of a witness; he'd been charged with using excessive force.

Yes, there was perhaps a technical reason for assigning Mikoyan—Allie was still on probation—but that didn't make it any less degrading.

Allie grimaced as he sipped the tin-tasting liquid. Then, too, alcohol had played a part in his suspension and probation. As the chief had told him, "One drink, Voegler, and it's bye-bye."

The jukebox was set on automatic and playing Patsy Cline, Dr. Nightingale's favorite singer. That was fine. Allie didn't even want to think about what his idiotic confession would do to his relationship with Didi. He could not bear another breakup with her, another fracture, another suspension. He could not bear the thought that she would not return to his apartment again, that she would not forgive, that she would not reward him for his honesty.

Suddenly there was a noise at the other end of the bar. He turned, looked, and cursed under his breath. It was that fool of a poet, Burt Conyers, dressed and looking as usual like a lunatic shepherd in from the hills—sheepskin vest, staff, mangled hair and beard, tattered sneakers. Didi liked him as an eccentric. Allie loathed him as a fraud.

Conyers had always proclaimed himself a poet, but no one in Hillsbrook believed him until an Albany public television station did a program on him and declared him to be an important rural poet in the Robert Frost tradition.

Since then, even though he never bathed and slept wherever he fell down each night, he had become a local literary celebrity, invited to various convocations and functions to open the ceremonies with a poem.

As for the poetry itself, it had a macabre pas-

toral bent. His poems were usually about dis-
eased trees or road kill or rutting deer or mush-
rooms as phallic images.

Conyers was also a drunk and Allie turned
quickly away, trying to avoid being solicited for
a drink.

But it was too late. Conyers had seen him.

The derelict poet approached and tapped Allie
on the shoulder.

"Yeah?" Allie asked nastily.

Conyers began to recite:

> Behold the wildflowers;
> Those sweet carpets of death;
> Suck in their light strychnine
> pollen . . .

"No more! Okay!" Allie called out, then ordered the bartender to take care of Conyers. The
poet smiled and watched intently as the man behind the bar poured him a shot of rye whiskey
and buttressed it with a bottle of Miller's.

The bartender collected the money from Allie.
Conyers started to babble. Allie hunched over to
ride it out.

His cell phone began to ring.

Relief! He walked into the shadows behind the
bend of the bar.

He heard Didi's voice. "Where are you?"

"In a bar. On Route 44," he answered quickly. He restrained himself. He wanted to cry out with joy that contact with her had been reestablished, the storm blown over. All he did say was: "Can you meet me somewhere now?"

She answered: "No. This is a business call."

Her voice had that icy politeness he had grown to fear. Like she was talking to a dairy farmer who hadn't paid his bill in a year.

There was a long pause. Neither of them spoke.

Allie thought: Can she hear the jukebox? Can she hear Patsy Cline?

"I need the name of a police officer in Albertsville," Didi said.

"Albertsville," he repeated dully, a bit confused.

"Yes. That's up on the Hudson in Greene County."

He made the connection. "That Zen retreat Rose burned down was in Albertsville."

Didi ignored his sudden enlightenment. Again that icy calm voice. "Give me a name, please."

"When can I see you again, Didi? I have to talk to you."

"A name."

"Okay. Raymond Buckle. He's not a cop anymore, but he still lives there. He had to quit. He was hurt in a hunting accident. I don't know what he does now."

"Thank you."

She hung up. Allie stared at the phone. He loathed the gadget. He flung it against the far wall.

After the sound of shattering plastic, he heard another sound. The poet was applauding the destruction by banging his staff against the bar railing.

"Bless all the Luddites!" he shouted.

Chapter 4

Six-thirty in the morning. Dr. Nightingale packed immediately after her yogic exercises and coffee. She packed one carryall with basic essentials.

Then she told her elves she was going for a long drive—maybe a week, maybe a month—and she would call them every other night. She claimed emotional distress as the impetus for her journey . . . the need to be alone for a while.

Then she went into her office, which had been added to the house for a small animal practice, and reprogrammed the phone to connect with her back-up vet, Randazzo. She also carefully packed a small chest with basic veterinary supplies pertaining to blood and tissue testing and three collapsible "have-a-heart" type traps.

She brought the supplies and her carryall out to the red Jeep, then returned to the house and walked upstairs into her mother's bedroom—the one she had inherited.

She sat down on her mother's rocking chair and took out the check that had been in the envelope—the envelope Charlie had received from Lily Black.

It was a cashier's check from a Chase Bank branch in downtown Manhattan, obtained by Rose Vigdor and made out to Deirdre Quinn Nightingale for $22,000.

Where had Rose gotten that kind of money? She was perpetually broke. She had spent every dime she had saved on the barn and the property.

What did Rose want her to do with it?

Should she send it to that aunt the police had uncovered?

Did Rose want her to give a wild wake for the people who had loved her? But who had loved her and whom had she loved?

Didi stared hard at the check. It was the saddest piece of paper she had ever held.

She closed her eyes and tried to pray. It was futile. She folded the check, put it into her wallet, and walked back out to the Jeep.

Twenty minutes later she was standing in Rose Vigdor's cavernous barn. Sunlight was filtering through new cracks in the ceiling beams.

It had been six months since Didi had been there; six months since she had discovered that Rose had loaded a few belongings and her dogs into her antique Volvo and left without a word to anyone.

Didi walked over to the potbellied wood-burning stove with the immense ugly grate. Rose had been so proud of it and of her ability to work it safely and efficiently.

For a moment Didi simply could not believe that Rose was dead. She would kill her? Who would want to kill her?

Sure, the natives of Hillsbrook always thought she was a bit around the bend. The fact that she had left a high-paying job in Manhattan to live like a "nature girl" in a drafty, unfinished barn with no electricity confirmed their belief in her irrationality. That she was tall and beautiful and blond made her even more suspect. But hate? The hate that kills? Never.

Didi kept turning slowly as if Rose were about to appear, calling out one of her endless supply of names for Didi: Nightgown, Nightingale, Night Train, Birdy, Doc, Bugs, Quinlan, Girl-friend, Lulubelle.

Then Didi's gaze caught one of the rolled-up mats that Rose had used on the barn floor.

Was that the one on which Rose and Allie had made love?

She felt a sudden rage. Had her whole friendship with Rose been bogus?

Had Rose really hated her? Felt contempt for her? Used her?

What other explanation could there be for Rose's behavior with Allie? Or for the fact that she had left Hillsbrook so suddenly without telling her?

Or for the fact that she had visited Lily Black in Hillsbrook only a month ago, and not even called Didi?

Or for the fact that she was obviously in some kind of bad trouble but had not asked Didi for help?

And then the rage dissipated.

Didi felt her loss and confusion so palpably that she had to steady herself by holding onto the stove.

She stared up at the morning light filtering through the roof. Fantastic images began to play in her mind. Rose, in her Guatemalan poncho, fleeing Hillsbrook with her dogs running behind her; Rose, her face blackened like an Army Ranger, torching a Zen retreat; Rose, desperate, begging for her life from a madman with a shovel.

Didi walked swiftly out of the barn and climbed into the Jeep. As she switched on the ignition to begin her journey to Albertsville, she had the sudden desire to set fire to Rose's barn. The ludicrousness of such an idea quickly shamed her into calmness and resolve.

The elves were stunned by Dr. Nightingale's unexpected departure—so quick . . . so dramatic . . . so irresponsible.

Usually when she went on a trip, she left detailed written instructions on a variety of matters. Not this time.

"Maybe," Trent Tucker suggested, "she'll drive a few miles, feel better, and turn around and come back."

"And maybe my feet won't hurt this evening," noted a contemptuous Mrs. Tunney.

Abigail supported her by banging a teaspoon on her coffee cup.

It was now 7 A.M., far later than they ever remained at the breakfast table, but they were absorbed in their benefactor's plight.

All except Charlie Gravis. He put on a sad face so as not to provoke Mrs. Tunney, but he wasn't thinking at all about Doc's sudden departure. He was contemplating the fact that for the first time in almost a week he had not had that miserable dream.

Did that mean he was no longer subject to the coming horrors that Lily Black had said were predicted by the dream?

He looked at Mrs. Tunney with an earnest expression as she launched into one of her pet theories that everything bad that happened to Didi and her environs could be blamed on her evil boyfriend. She believed that Officer Albert Voegler was the closest thing to Satan in Hillsbrook.

Charlie kept nodding his head as if in agreement, all the while wondering how he could get back to Lily Black as soon as possible. Ike was not available this morning to drive him.

It would have to be Trent Tucker, Charlie realized. He was uncomfortable going anywhere with the young man because Trent was a fast, irresponsible driver who liked to corner his pickup as if it were a sports car.

But, Charlie thought, only the rich have choices.

Mrs. Tunney made one final short monologue about how prayer could possibly keep the child safe—the child being Didi. Prayer and nutrition and something called levity—Charlie never knew what it meant and believed Mrs. Tunney did not know either, but she did love the word.

After the breakfast club disbanded, Charlie asked Trent for a ride to Lily Black's. Trent happily agreed and off they went.

As usual, they drove together in total silence. Charlie had absolutely nothing to say to the young man and vice versa. At least, there was no enmity between them.

When they reached the Black place, Charlie ordered him: "Wait here for me."

Lily was out back, hanging up wet clothes on a old-fashioned line. The terriers didn't charge this time; they just growled.

"Back again?" she queried, smiling.

There was no breeze at all on that warm summer morning, but the woman's hair was out of its bun and blowing free. Yes, it was actually blowing as if there was a brisk breeze. Charlie thought: How could a woman this old have such long, lustrous hair?

She kept hanging the clothes with wooden clothespins.

It occurred to Charlie that he had forgotten the first name of her dead husband, even though Ike had said they both knew the dairy farmer Black well.

"Can I call you Lily?"

"Of course." She cocked her head quizzically. "Did you have another dream, Charlie?"

"No, no. In fact I came here because my other dream has vanished."

"Dreams usually do."

"I mean, what I want to know is . . . if it has gone with the wind—poof, vanished—does your prediction vanish? I mean, if the cow is dead, it can't calve."

"True."

"And she can't give any more milk."

"True."

"So, Lily, what about it? What about . . ."

He tried hard to remember her exact words, so strange on the lips, like poems—and then they came to him in a burst and he recited them: "violent demise and fond remembrance."

The utterance exhausted him.

"Dreams are not cows," Lily said.

"So it's going to happen."

"I may have been wrong. Who knows? But I am often right," she said, playing meditatively with a clothespin.

He felt dread. He also had a sudden desire to touch Lily's head . . . and her hair.

"So even if I never get the dream again . . . even if I forget the dream . . . it will happen."

"Yes. If I interpreted the dream correctly."

"Can you tell me what the words mean?"

"What words?"

"Violent demise and fond remembrance."

"Get a dictionary, Charlie."

"I'm too old for dictionaries. Anyway . . . I mean . . . how will it happen? I mean, which way will the rabbit jump?"

"Come inside, Charlie, and have something to drink."

"No! I have to get back!"

He walked away. He stopped, turned, and walked back close to her.

"Is life hard for you now?" he asked.

"Yes. Very hard. Very lonely."

He kissed her quickly and gently on the top of her head. It seemed like the most natural thing in the world, although he had not made a gesture like that for some fifty-odd years. He felt no shame, no lust, no discomfort, no exultation.

"When am I gonna die, Lily?" he whispered. "And who is going to remember me?"

"Oh, Charlie . . . don't you want something cool to drink?"

His manner changed. He said a curt good-bye and returned to the truck.

Dr. Nightingale drove through the tiny village of Albertsville: a pretty young woman in a dusty red Jeep, with short black hair and wearing a very washed-out flannel shirt and jeans along with inexpensive running shoes and no socks. She had a short, compact build that made her seem larger and heavier than she really was.

Everyone called Deirdre Nightingale good-looking, but no one ever called her beautiful, and a lot of people considered her hard or mean or flippant. She was none of those; she was simply overwhelmed, often, even though she had carefully nurtured a personal myth of fearlessness and competence in veterinary medicine.

The village she was driving through had a bank but no formal post office. It had a grocery and a hair cutter and a general store of sorts where newspapers could be purchased.

Albertsville was old and crumbling, but one could see new houses on the slopes surrounding the village. The village itself was only half a mile from the Hudson and access to the river was an old trunk road from abandoned gravel quarries. The road connected to County Highway 9A, which ran north and south along the great river on its eastern bank.

When she reached Sunyata House, Didi sat in the Jeep and stared—dazed and appalled.

The fire had obviously been severe. Nothing was left of the large two-story nineteenth-century house but its stone foundation. Even the clump of trees in which it had been situated and the spacious lawn that led down to the riverbank were charred an ugly gray.

Rose, if it was Rose, had done the job well. Rose, or Sonya, if she indeed was Sonya Loomis at the time, had shown no mercy. She had to have hated mightily to do it so thoroughly and carefully; amateur arsonists usually bungled the job. And this was no bungle. This was annihilation.

When had Mikoyan said the fire had happened? Two months ago?

Didi noticed evidence that rebuilding would begin shortly—stacks of wood, sacks, and sealed containers under tarpaulins.

She saw no one but an old man raking stones in the small circular parking lot.

Behind the remains of the house and a bit north was a large trailer; it looked like one of those special vehicles one sees when movies are being shot on location, the several doors and steps leading to dressing rooms.

Didi pulled the Jeep into the lot, got out, and approached the groundskeeper. She was nervous, but she knew exactly what she had to do.

"My name is Dr. Nightingale," she announced. "I'm doing rabies research for the New York State Department of Agriculture."

Didi flashed an ID card that identified her as such. It had been a valid ID three years ago, when she had in fact been so employed, but the date was not visible to the casual viewer.

"No rabies around here," said the man pleasantly, leaning on his tool. Then he added, "My name is John Maywood."

"It's a precautionary survey. I'm required to trap and test squirrels and muskrats in the area."

"Plenty of squirrels, miss. Don't see many muskrats."

"Is there a director about?"

"Up at the trailer. Name of Tim Arksit."

"What happened here?" Didi asked, pointing at the house.

"Fire. Bad fire."

"Anyone killed?"

"No. A few burns. But there's nothing left of the place."

"Sad," said Didi.

Maywood nodded. Didi walked to the trailer and knocked on the center door. She could see air-conditioners jutting out of the strange-looking windows.

"It's open," a voice called from inside.

She walked in. Three people were seated in the lounge area of the trailer. Everything was furnished in a minimalist, modular fashion. The inside walls were painted a light, restful tan.

"I'm looking for Tim Arksit," she said.

Lydia Adamson

"I'm he."

The speaker was a man in his sixties. Close-cut hair. Casual dress. Very trim and martial looking for his age, with bright blue eyes.

A woman of about forty was seated to his left. She was dressed as if she was about to garden. A pretty, blunt face with a very serious demeanor.

The other man in the trailer appeared to be much younger, about thirty. He was wearing sandals and shorts. His hair was long and black and his body was deeply tanned.

Didi went through the same routine with Arksit as she had with the caretaker in the parking lot. The director bought her story so quickly he didn't even look at the lapsed ID.

"Be my guest," he said, "but I must warn you, there will be construction workers and activity on the premises."

"I understand."

Arksit smiled, a false smile, indicating that the interview was over.

She turned and started out. Her eyes caught a batch of Sunyata House brochures on a small table under the wall phone.

"Mind if I take one?" she asked.

"Please do," said Arksit.

Brochure in hand, Didi returned to the Jeep. She felt exhilarated. The rabies ruse had worked

50

to perfection. She could now wander the premises at will.

It took her only twenty minutes to locate a motel outside of Albertsville—within walking distance of both the village and Sunyata House. It was called the River Motel and it consisted of twelve very small bungalows in a circle around an office.

Didi brought her bags in and fell down on the bed. She was exhausted. She leafed leisurely through the descriptive brochure.

"An interdenominational oasis in which to achieve wisdom and peace," the brochure said. "Activities based on Zenist principles of meditation."

There were many photos in the brochure— staff, grounds, classes in session—including several of saffron-robed Buddhist monks from abroad visiting their western lay counterparts.

From the photos, Didi quickly realized that the woman in the trailer was Serena Babbington, the head of the "Sitting Zen" retreat program. Here, students sat in meditation under the guidance of instructors and tried to extinguish all cravings and thoughts and mindfulness in order to reach "no-mind," wherein all the dust is removed from the mirror of the mind.

The young man in the trailer was identified in

the brochure as Dan Campari, head of the "Walking Zen" program, where the retreatants meditated and chanted while walking slowly in a column.

The applicant could stay as long as he or she wished. Food and lodging and instruction at either "Sitting Zen" or "Walking Zen" were provided at $700 per week.

Didi was astonished at the high cost. And this would probably rise after the Sunyata House was rebuilt. How did Rose afford the price?

Didi dropped the brochure over the side of the bed. She had to nap. At least for an hour. Then she could look for that former cop, Raymond Buckle. She felt satisfied. She knew she was where she was supposed to be.

Chapter 5

"You have to calm down," Ike Badian counseled his friend.

They were having a beer in the town pub, which, except for them, was empty at noon.

Charlie Gravis was clearly agitated, and acting so, climbing up and down off the barstool in spite of his arthritic limbs, twirling his beer stein, grumbling and cursing at nothing in particular.

"Why do I have to calm down, Ike? I'll be dead soon, right? Then I'll be calm in the grave for seven billion years. That's how long this earth is going to last. And then—boom!—the sun goes out."

Ike did not respond. He sipped his beer.

"That damned fortune teller of yours, Ike . . ."

Badian interrupted angrily. "She's not my fortune teller. She's yours. You had the dream. I just fixed you up with her."

"Okay, okay. But listen. She won't tell me what the violent demise is. I went to see her the other morning."

"What is there to tell, Charlie? She says you're gonna die."

"Yeah, I know that. But *when?* And *how?* I mean, if I know, I can—"

"No! I know what you're thinking, Charlie. But if she's right, you can't head it off. At least I don't think so."

Charlie thought for a long time. Then he said, "You know, Ike, I think I agree with you about this. I can't head VD off."

"What's this VD?"

"You stupid? Violent demise. VD. So, let me get back to my point, Ike. I could get a heart attack right now, it could be one of those violent ones where you start shaking and bouncing and gasping and then you're dead. Or it could be when I walk out of here I get hit by a bakery truck."

"Sure."

"But I think this Black lady is talking about something else. Like a bomb or a conflagration. You know what I mean?"

"Sure."

"There are a thousand possibilities."

"Damn right, Charlie."

"So I think when all is said and done, I should forget about VD and calm down and deal with FR."

"What the hell is FR?"

"What's the matter with you, Ike? Your memory is like a sieve. Fond remembrance."

"Okay."

"So I ask you, Ike. Who do you know that's going to remember me fondly?"

"Me, I guess. And maybe a few others."

"Sure, for five minutes. No! I think the dream meant something else. That the whole world will have a fond remembrance of me."

"You better leave the rest of that beer alone, Charlie."

The agitation and the confusion and even the years seemed to suddenly slip away from Charlie Gravis. He laughed and slapped his friend hard on the back and then yelled to the bartender, "Whiskey!"

Then he bent over and whispered in Ike's ear: "Believe me, Ike, all this carrying on by me about the VD and the FR don't mean nothing. I'm beyond that. I've crossed over the river. I have started 'Cows and Me.'"

"What is that?"

"My memoirs—the memoirs of a dairy farmer. When the VD hits, I hope to have it finished. I'm writing like a demon. But listen, Ike, whenever it comes—I mean the VD—get the pages from my room and get them published. I mean, Ike, they're dynamite. The true story. The FR is really gonna flow. Fifty percent butterfat, at least. Hey?"

Ike Badian sank deeper into his barstool. There was not much he could do.

Allie Voegler sat in his usual booth in the Hillsbrook Diner—the last one in the window aisle, near the pay phone.

Now he carried a cell phone. He didn't have to sit near a pay phone at all, but the habit persisted.

There was a substitute waitress on duty who didn't know him. She actually handed him a menu. He gave it back immediately and ordered pancakes and sausages.

It was such a strange order for a late afternoon meal that the waitress hesitated, thinking perhaps the customer was joking with her. Then, when no revision was forthcoming, she left with the order. For some people, she thought, breakfast never ends.

In addition to the pancakes, Allie was looking forward to some reflection and repose—but all he got was the state trooper Mikoyan, who seemed to materialize out of thin air and sat down across from him with a "May I?"

Then he ordered a cup of coffee and asked Allie, "Are you eating now?"

"I am."

"I mean, did you order already?"

"Yes."

"Okay. Look, after you eat, I need another favor."

"We're all in this together. What do you need?"

"A ride to the Nightingale place. I have to talk to that young vet again."

"About what?"

Allie tried hard to keep his voice level, his manner disinterested.

"Well, I've been hearing rumors that Rose Vigdor was seen hanging around Hillsbrook before she was murdered."

"So?"

"So that Nightingale woman claimed to be Rose's best friend. It doesn't make sense that Rose wouldn't contact her."

"No, it doesn't," Allie agreed, in principle.

The pancakes came. Allie ate slowly. Mikoyan read the Hillsbrook paper. They didn't say another word to each other.

Then Voegler drove the homicide detective out to the Nightingale property. Mrs. Tunney answered his knock on the front door very slowly. When she finally swung the door open and saw that it was Voegler—a man she did not like— and the visitor who had been in her kitchen, she slipped on one of her blank, stupid old lady masks.

"How can I help you?"

Mikoyan said, "I'm looking for Deirdre Nightingale."

"Who?"

"Dr. Deirdre Quinn Nightingale. Don't you remember me?"

Mrs. Tunney shook her head no. The yard dogs were now sticking their heads closer to the open door. She narrowed the door to prevent their access and said, "She's not here. She went away for a few days."

"Where?"

Mrs. Tunney noted that A. Voegler had not uttered a single word.

"I don't know. There must have been some sick animal somewhere. Maybe a whole lot of them. That's what Miss Quinn does. She treats sick animals. She goes all over the land and treats sick animals. She treats cows and dogs and pigs and horses and even gray parrots, if you have one."

"Do you know when she's coming back?"

"No."

Mikoyan produced a business card from his wallet and handed it to Mrs. Tunney. "When you speak to her, please give her my number. Tell her I'm waiting for her call. It's important."

Mrs. Tunney slammed the door shut. The two men walked back to the car. Allie was filled with consternation. It had never occurred to him when he gave Didi the name of that ex cop in Albertsville that she would actually go there. But now he was sure that was where she had gone. Why would she do that? He tried to come up with answers, but he could think of only two reasons for her journey. And both of them were unacceptable.

One—she simply wanted to get away from him.

Two—she wanted to unearth the last months of her friend's life before Rose became a corpse in a shallow Hillsbrook grave.

Allie climbed into his car. His shirt was wringing wet with sweat. Mikoyan climbed in beside him.

Allie lit a cigarette and asked, "You want to go back to town?"

"Yes."

Allie kept smoking. He didn't turn the ignition on.

"She's a strange duck, isn't she?" Mikoyan asked.

"You mean the Tunney woman?"

"No. I mean the Nightingale woman."

Allie didn't agree or disagree.

Mikoyan continued, "I mean, everything about her is strange. The way she never sent in a missing person report after her friend vanished. The way she just ups and leaves now, like her dead friend did. The way she treats her people. Am I right or not?"

Voegler did not answer. He took one last drag of the cigarette, flung it out of the window, and started the car.

"Do you know her?" Mikoyan asked suddenly, quietly.

Allie realized the state trooper had moved into a difficult line of inquiry. The inflection in his voice was totally different. Allie had to be careful.

"I know almost everybody in Hillsbrook," he replied.

"I mean, intimately."

"Hard to say."

"Did you sleep with her?"

"There again, that's a funny expression. It covers a whole variety of things."

"Did you have any kind of consensual sex with her?"

"Yes. I suppose I did."

"Why didn't you tell me?"

"You didn't ask."

"Anything else you got to tell me?"

"No."

"You know where she went?"

"No," Allie lied.

"Do you know anything about the Rose Vigdor murder that you have not revealed to the department or to me?"

"No."

Mikoyan shook his head in disgust, then coughed and spat out the window.

"Look, Voegler, I understand your resentment. This should be your case. But I was called in. So let's be goddamn professional about it. I need your help."

"You got it."

"But you're not offering anything. You're not giving me anything to work with."

"Like what?"

"Like who in Hillsbrook hated this Rose Vigdor or Sonya Loomis or any other name she might have used."

"No one hated her."

"Then who loved her?"

61

"Dr. Nightingale," replied Allie.

He pulled a small folded piece of paper out of his shirt pocket and handed it to Mikoyan.

The state trooper perused it and asked, "Who are these people?"

"A list of everyone in Hillsbrook who knew her well, if anyone knew her well."

Mikoyan read the list again. He smiled. "You're not on it," he noted.

"Why should I be?"

It wasn't difficult finding Raymond Buckle. He was in the area phone book. His house was small, freshly painted black and yellow, and it stood alone in a field of shrub oak on the outskirts of the village.

The moment he opened the door, Didi said, "Albert Voegler from Hillsbrook gave me your name."

He ushered her in rather gallantly. Didi immediately noticed that, unlike Allie's other acquaintances, he did not instantly evaluate her figure for erotic possibilities.

The right side of his face and neck was disfigured.

Even obvious plastic surgery had not been able to make it visually palatable.

His right arm was also damaged; it hung like a sock from his shoulder.

Buckle was a short, powerfully built man in his early thirties. He had a large shock of dull red hair flecked with gray. He looked like a mournful, innocent farm boy.

The house was filled with hunting trophies along the walls—deer antlers and bear heads—and several rifles also hung on wall racks.

Didi remembered what Allie had told her—Buckle had been hurt in a hunting accident.

She tried not to stare at his face, but it was virtually impossible; she found herself sneaking small, intense peeks.

He picked up on it quickly.

The moment she sat down, at his invitation, on an old chair with a rattan back, he sat down on a similar chair across from her and said, "You get used to it. It could have been worse. We were turkey hunting. My partner was drunk. He forgot to put the safety on. He tripped over his own feet. Both barrels got me. The range was as close as you and me now. At that range the buckshot scalds as well as penetrates."

After he spoke he had to rest. He breathed in and out, hard.

Then he asked, "What can I do for you, miss?"

"Call me Didi. I need information about a

friend of mine who lived in the Albertsville area. Her name was Rose Vigdor."

"Never heard the name."

Didi pressed on. "Tall. Good-looking. Blonde. Dressed like a hippie, I suppose. Three dogs."

"Sorry. Don't know her." He laughed gently. "Would have liked to," he added.

"She may have used the name Sonya Loomis."

He sat up sharply. "Oh! Well, yeah! The woman who burned down Sunyata House."

"Then you knew her?"

"Not really. I think I saw her a few times in the village, but I don't remember your description. How did the hippies dress? All I know about her is what I heard after the crime."

"What did you hear?"

"She was staying at the place, taking classes or courses or whatever you call them. One night she brings in a case of Molotov cocktails—gasoline—lights the soaked rags at the top, and flings them against the walls. The place had bamboo shades. Went up fast, real fast. Sad. And I heard the place was wildly underinsured."

"Anyone find out why she did it?"

"There was an investigation. Nothing. No fights. No unhappiness. No grudges. It didn't make sense."

It was early evening but still light and there

were slivers of light dancing on the floor between their two chairs. He was wearing, she noticed, old army fatigues.

"I'm making some soup," he said. He laughed. "In summer I make hot soup. In winter, cold soup. I guess I'm a bit peculiar. Want some?"

"Sure."

He went into his kitchen, opened two cans of Progresso Escarole and Chicken Broth using his left hand and a wall electric can opener, poured the contents into a pot, and started heating it.

Didi looked around the house. Except for the spotless trophies on the wall, it was dusty and unkempt. The dining room table, and all the other furniture, was covered with newspapers, books, and magazines.

He came back with two bowls and handed her one. "How is Allie doing?" he asked.

"Fine."

"We used to hunt deer together in Delaware County. We keep in touch."

Didi sipped her soup. It was not hot enough, but she didn't complain.

"Why are you asking all these questions?"

"Rose Vigdor was my friend. She might well have been the woman Sonya Loomis. She was murdered in Hillsbrook. I'm not doing my own criminal investigation. I'm not a police officer. Maybe you could call it a pilgrimage."

"Yes. I understand. I wish I could help you but I'm not in contact with anyone, any more."

He is quite nice, Didi thought. Almost gentle. Surely not the kind of man who usually befriends Albert Voegler.

"What did people here think of Sunyata House?" she asked.

"Are you sure you're not a cop?"

"I'm a veterinarian."

He found that funny. He didn't seem to believe her but he answered the question.

"People around here liked the place. Sure, everyone thinks it's a kind of gentle fraud for people with too much money and time on their hands. And no one takes anything that goes on there in a serious—a spiritual—sense, but . . ."

He stopped suddenly, took out a handkerchief, and pressed it against the side of his mouth. He looked in pain.

Didi had some more soup and waited. She kept her eyes averted from his discomfort.

When he recovered, he said, "The people who run it seem okay. Look, there are a dozen such retreat houses up and down the Hudson within twenty miles of here. Some Buddhist, some

Hindu, some Christian, some New Age—and some that can't even be defined."

He hadn't touched his soup again. He excused himself, came back with a bottle of ale, and poured it into a glass, then drank a little at a time. He was sweating heavily even though the house was quite cool for the season.

I should leave now, Didi thought; there is nothing he can really tell me. But she didn't. There was something attractive about the man. She wondered what kind of books he was reading— one had the sense that even though he looked and acted like an overgrown farm boy, he had exotic interests.

No, she thought, it is definitely time to leave. "I have to go now. I appreciate your help."

"If I think of anything else, where can I reach you, miss?"

"At the River Motel."

He laughed, which was painful for him to do, and Didi didn't have to ask why he laughed. That motel had probably been the scene of half the youthful indiscretions in Albertsville.

"Anything you come up with would be helpful. Anything about her or her dogs."

"What dogs?" he inquired.

"She must have come to Albertsville with her two German shepherds and her Corgi. She never went anywhere without her dogs, I don't care what name she used."

"Sunyata House does not allow pets of any kind."

Didi froze in her tracks. This was very strange. Rose must have boarded them somewhere—somewhere close—where she could visit them frequently. Rose would not abandon them in any sense, for any amount of time, for any reason. But would Sonya?

She thought: One thing this Buckle had given her was the certainty that Mikoyan was right. Buckle had kind of paid for her trip. Loomis and Vigdor were most likely one and the same. In body, at least. But perhaps, when Rose became Sonya, she lost Rose-like qualities.

Was it Sonya who had slept with Allie?

This question opened up a whole new area of speculation.

Had this Rose-Sonya become some kind of soldier in a holy war?

Like Carswell, she thought.

The moment the name Carswell popped into her head, she felt stupid.

Carswell was a dog, a beagle.

He had cut himself badly on some barbed wire, going where he wasn't supposed to go. She had treated the dog successfully, but for some reason the local freezing agent she had used as an anesthetic had not worked very well. Carswell blamed her for his suffering, as well he might, although he had gotten himself into his own trouble.

After the treatment, he recovered quickly, but he would set upon her or her red Jeep any time he caught sight of her in Hillsbrook. Anywhere, any time, under any circumstances—he attacked.

A wonderful thought superceded thoughts of Carswell. No dogs in Albertsville—no Rose Vigdor. And no Rose means no Sonya, in spite of all the other circumstantial connections and identifications.

"You seem tired," she heard Raymond Buckle saying. "Would you like to stay for dinner?"

The light outside was fading and when Buckle asked her that question, he tilted his face so that the strange, contorted side took up the fading light like a blotter and it suddenly glowed. She had a sudden desire to put her hand on the face—like she would do sometimes with a fractious horse in pain. Ah, the vet in me, she thought. Always hands-on.

"I really can't, but thank you very much for the invitation. Tell me, are there any kennels in the area that board dogs?"

"Only one I know of. About a mile from your

motel, on the same road. A couple owns the place. Mr. and Mrs. Hanly. They used to breed Siberian huskies."

With his left hand he drew her a map on the back of a hunting magazine. His movements were halting; obviously, left was not his natural hand.

She thanked him again.

"How do you know Allie?" he finally asked.

"You mean, what is our relationship?"

"Oh," he said suddenly, in a self-deprecating manner, "this is none of my business. Please visit me again when you need anything."

It was a ten-minute drive to the Hanly place—a brooding piece of bare, hilly property on which stood a sprawling single-level house and three separate sets of kennel runs in a semicircle far behind the house. There were no animals about and she could see that the runs were all now in some disrepair.

They were a sweet old couple, a bit frightened—of what, she didn't know—and they cooperated happily, eagerly, when Didi flashed the expired ID.

Yes, they said, a woman named Rose Vigdor had rented a run for several weeks. Yes, she had three dogs—two shepherds and a Corgi.

When told the woman was dead and that Didi had to check the runs because two of her dogs had become rabid, they pointed out the exact run Rose had rented and visited every day.

They gave Didi carte blanche to investigate, and they even provided her with a large, wide-beam flashlight.

The unit in question had six runs, each one encased in wire, each one ending in a covered shed where the dogs could seek shelter during bad weather.

It was a beautiful summer night. In spite of the brief, intense nap at the motel, Didi was still bone-tired.

She also realized she had really gotten the information she came for. The nut . . . the essentials . . . Rose Vigdor was the arsonist Sonya Loomis. The dogs' stay here proved it beyond a shadow of a doubt no matter her own hopeful alternative scenarios.

The rest was really for the police. They were the ones investigating the murder. As for the $22,000 check from Rose, that too was for the police.

All she could and should do was go back home and mourn—not only the horrid deaths of Rose and the shepherds, but her own stupidity at not knowing who Rose truly was.

She flicked off the flashlight. Why look for evidence of the dogs' stay here? The old couple had no reason to lie.

Didi hesitated, then flicked the light on again and scanned the runs, more to support her rabies ruse than out of any hope of finding confirming data.

At the third run, the beam fell on what she recognized as Aretha's feeding bowl.

Or was it?

She opened the gate and walked down the run until she stood over the bowl. It seemed to be Aretha's. But why would Rose leave the bowl? She was very protective of her dog's feeding utensils.

Didi continued into the covered shed.

There was a shelf along one wall and on that shelf were six cans of beef dinners for dogs and two bags of dry dog food.

Didi flicked the light off. This was confusing. Rose did not feed her dogs commercial food—just raw meat and an organic mix of chopped greens and cooked grains, usually oats.

Maybe other dogs had used the kennel since Rose had rented it. But there was no evidence of that. Maybe the couple had forgotten which kennel runs Rose had rented.

She shone the light again on the feeding bowl. No, that was definitely Aretha's bowl. Blue metal, high sides, a yellow design around the rim. Each of Rose's dogs had his or her own distinctive bowl. Poor Aretha—a gentle, wise, old German shepherd who looked after everyone and ended up in a ditch.

Didi decided to take down the dog food and bring it to the Hanlys. They probably didn't know it was there. They might be able to use it.

As she brought down the bags of dry food, she realized that one of them was quite light. Maybe there was only a cupful of dry food left. She shook the bag.

It didn't sound like dry food. It sounded like paper.

She dumped the contents of the bag onto the ground.

She saw two thick packets, each one fastened with a rubber band. She removed the rubber band on the first pack.

Thirteen individual maps of the Hudson River and environs. Cheap road maps. Expensive detail maps. Very old maps. Historical maps depicting battles. Exotic geological survey maps. Antique maps.

Some of them covered the entire length of the Hudson from New York City to Canada. Some covered only small stretches of the river. Some covered the entire state from east to west as well as north and south as the river lies.

Didi didn't know what to make of them. If these were indeed Rose's, what was going on? Had she been thinking of rafting the whole river, or becoming a river pilot?

She took the rubber band off the second pack. It consisted of seven small manila envelopes, the kind that folded legal documents like leases are often mailed in.

Each envelope was addressed to Sonya Loomis at a post office box in Albertsville.

The return address on each envelope was the same—J. Benedict on West 110th Street in Manhattan.

Each envelope contained three sheets of white paper. Two of the sheets were blank and the third always had the same three-line message: "Dear Rose, Be well. Love, Joan."

And that was it.

Every packet was exactly the same in the way it was addressed, the number of sheets, and the message.

Didi flicked the light off. What did the maps and letters mean?

Why had Rose left them? Who was this Joan Benedict?

Why had this Benedict sent Rose these bizarre

three-page letters, with only those three lines repeated on the first page of each letter?

A cold shiver went through Didi.

Why had Rose left Aretha's bowl?

Because she was running? Because she was in fear for her life?

Or had her terrible act of firebombing so deranged her that she forgot to gather all her belongings? Or had she been deranged before that?

Why leave only one feeding bowl?

How did someone in New York City know that Rose was using the name Sonya Loomis in Albertsville? Someone whom Rose had never mentioned to Didi.

Didi knew one thing for sure: Suddenly she was not ready to go back home yet.

Chapter 6

Charlie Gravis had slept about three hours the whole night—from 10 P.M. to 1 A.M.

From one to six he had completed the first chapter, thirty-four pages, of his great work, "Cows and Me."

He had obtained the pencils and paper from Dr. Nightingale's office, which was situated in her small animal clinic.

The paper was actually the backs of large white envelopes constantly being sent to Dr. Nightingale with lab results and X-rays in them.

The pencils had a thick black lead.

He figured that it would be best to start out with his relationship to cows and save the stuff about the mechanisms and economics of the dairy farmer's life for later on in the book.

Charlie was astonished at how easy it had been to write, and also fun. Of course, it was a bit fatiguing, but that was immediately overcome by the exultation at spinning out a few fine thoughts.

In this, the first chapter, he had concentrated on his unique perspective on the mind and soul of the cow. After all—who knew cows better than he!

He realized, as he was writing faster and faster, that some of his prose was a bit flowery. But ah, what insights! At least he thought they were insights. How most cows, for example, were sweet and sly. How the few mean ones were kind of dumb, which made them not too dangerous. How being kicked by a cow really didn't hurt that much and very seldom was a bone broken. How he once kicked a cow back. How when he finally installed milking machines he started to sing to the cows . . . a repertoire of maybe five songs . . . one of them, "I Left My Heart in San Francisco," had turned out to be the cows' favorite.

Yes, he got down all kinds of good stuff like that in a frenzy of memory.

When 6 A.M. came, he went to breakfast with the others and positively gobbled down Mrs. Tunney's glutinous oatmeal, plus a boiled egg, plus two pieces of toast with plum jam.

Everyone remarked about his newly found robust appetite and how chipper he was. Charlie did not explain. How could he!

They would get depressed if he told them about his soon-to-happen violent demise. They would scoff at the dream and its interpretation, claiming that all old people think death is imminent and sometimes it is and sometimes it isn't and the dreams they have are about as predictive as how many pies of cow manure will be in a given field.

And they would not understand or appreciate the fond remembrance he was creating.

When he returned to his tiny room, he sat on the edge of the bed and carefully read what he had written.

My my my. It took his breath away. It would be a book for the ages. No doubt about it.

He leaned back, closed his eyes, and gently fantasized. Maybe a hundred years in the future, a young man on a farm on some distant space station would be reading, enjoying, and learning from the classic "Cows and Me" by Charlie Gravis.

Oh, this was fond remembrance indeed! God bless Lily for telling him the truth.

Reality nudged him a bit. He ought to show the pages to someone to confirm his belief in their exceptional quality.

Who? Ike? No way! Ike was sorry he ever brought his friend to the dream lady. And he really didn't believe a word of the prediction. Ike was his only friend, but a fool was a fool.

The only one he could think of was Harland Frick.

Now, Frick was old, even older than he probably. But he was still sharp as a tack. He was the owner of a healthy food store in town, a tiny man with broken blood vessels on his nose and tufts of white hair dotting his almost bald skull.

A lot of people considered him eccentric, and he was, but Charlie had always respected him. Frick knew more about the Hillsbrook area than anyone else. He knew the history of the people and the places. And he knew where the skeletons were. Charlie liked him better than most people. He used to drink with Harland out in the Highway Pub. After three whiskeys Harland would begin to say peculiar things. This mild, very well-mannered shopkeeper would hiss out his hatred for a whole lot of people—mostly newcomers to Hillsbrook with money, and old-timers who sold their dairy farms to the invaders. But the next morning Harland wouldn't remember a word he'd said, and if you told him what he'd said, he would think you were pulling his leg.

Yes, Charlie would show his writing to Harland Frick.

At ten o'clock in the morning he persuaded Trent Tucker to drive him into town.

At ten-thirty he walked into Frick's store and found to his chagrin that the poet Burt Conyers was also paying the proprietor a visit. In fact, they were drinking coffee together.

Charlie, still remembering Conyers's role in his latest entrepreneurial debacle, snarled at the poet, but Conyers seemed to take no offense at all.

Frick, ever the genial host, made a cup of coffee for Charlie also and they all sat down on large unopened cartons of organic chips.

Charlie had the envelopes—on the backs of which he had composed his first chapter—rolled up and fastened with a rubber band. He kept plucking the rubber band like a banjo string until Harland asked slyly, "What are you hiding there, Charlie?"

That was all Charlie needed. He ripped the rubber band off, unrolled the large white envelopes with the pencil jottings on one side, and thrust them into Harland's hands.

"I am writing a book," Charlie announced.

"Too little, too late," quipped the derelict rural poet.

Charlie ignored him. He said to Harland, "I just want you to read what I got."

"Delighted," said Harland Frick.

The reading began. Charlie and Burt sat quietly, side by side, waiting.

For the first time since he walked in, Charlie noticed that directly behind Harland's head was the glass case that held organic eggs from the freest running chickens in New York State. Or so the ridiculous sign read.

Then he saw Harland's eyes smiling. Oh! He knew the man would appreciate it! He knew!

Then Harland put the sheaf of envelopes down, rolled them up carefully, and handed them back to Charlie.

"Incredible," Harland said.

"Thank you."

"Who would ever believe that our own Charlie Gravis, not a spring chicken I may add, has written one of the best children's books I have ever read."

Children's book?

Charlie felt as if he had been hit in the face by a blunt object.

"Are you serious, Harland?" he whispered.

"Damn right, Charlie. I mean, I'd give it to my great-granddaughter in a minute. I'd give it to her for Christmas. Hell, I'd even give it to her for her birthday!"

"Children are like rabid chipmunks in the attic," noted Burt, and then added, "I know a children's book illustrator in Rhinebeck. She draws like an ecstatic garden hose. She'll work for you, Charlie."

Charlie, clutching his manuscript, staggered out.

Once on the street, he leaned against the building. He felt humiliated and embarrassed. He thought he had begun a classic that would live as long as men milk cows. Instead, he had created a silly little children's book.

He felt dizzy. He pressed his head against the wall for a moment of repose . . . and then, gathering strength, ripped the envelopes apart in a fury and scattered the pieces into the soft summer breeze.

He walked unsteadily to the pub. It was not open. He walked to the stationery store, which also sold lottery tickets, and read the list of recent winning numbers.

This calmed him, steadied him, strengthened him. He walked out and began to window shop along the village street. He stopped in front of the shoe store. There was a sale in progress on summer stuff, like sandals and deck shoes.

Then, right there, being a mature man, he regained his composure and realized that his literary delusions were not fatal. They were not the VD and in fact they were—these delusions—extremely instructive. He had gained wisdom. No doubt about it.

He started to walk again through the village, a bit jauntily. He knew he would have to set his sights lower, much, much lower.

Back to a one-person fond remembrance, probably.

This, of course, led him back into the cul de sac of there really being no one to remember him fondly.

And that was when he had a truly profound thought, and it bit deep.

Dr. Deirdre Quinn Nightingale.

As things stood now, she would probably remember him fondly for forty-eight hours.

But that was his fault, not hers.

Maybe, if he acted correctly, she would remember him as long as she treated animals.

Tears came to Charlie's eyes.

Hadn't she rescued him from the tyranny of Mrs. Tunney and employed him as a legitimate veterinary assistant?

Hadn't she ignored his foibles, his prejudices, his cantankerousness—and kept him on and given his sad, bankrupt life some kind of meaning?

Shouldn't he give her something valuable that would keep the FR going after his VD—which might come any moment now?

He was swept by memories of Doc and him. Like a moving picture film. He wondered if they had become a famous couple in the county—a kind of weird Bonnie and Clyde—riding the hills in their red chariot, looking for sick beasts in the fields.

An old memory came back to him with such force that he had to balance himself against a parking sign.

It was early on in their partnership, soon after Doc had come back home to practice. They went to a fancy pig farm near the Connecticut border. The owner of the place was a rich idiot with crazy hog-breeding ideas. Two of his big Yorkshire sows were sick.

Doc examined them. She couldn't make a diagnosis. Then she asked the breeder to leave.

"Why?" he asked angrily. "They're my pigs."

She smiled and said, "Yes, they are. But before I start doing some tests, I want to talk to them privately."

Yes, sometimes Doc Nightingale was a card.

But she was also young, tough, pretty, kind, and a helluva vet.

Charlie Gravis suddenly knew what he had to do to ensure the longest lasting FR possible.

He would find the killer of her friend Rose Vigdor.

Then he realized he had forgotten which corner he was supposed to be picked up on by Trent Tucker for the ride back.

Didi arrived at Sunyata House, or what was left of it, early in the morning, rested and re-solved to do . . . what?

She really didn't know, but she would do something . . . and she would flash a few of those strange Hudson River maps.

The caretaker was already about the premises when she arrived. As Didi set her traps to cover the bogus assignment, the old caretaker, whose name she had forgotten, kept chatting on. "I never seen a squirrel trap baited with peanut butter on crackers. But then again, squirrels love nuts, so why not peanut butter? I guess you know best, miss. This is a government assignment, right? Hell, you might be CIA. I better keep my mouth shut."

Didi kept her eyes on the trailer as she worked.

The woman appeared first—Serena Babbington.

Then came Arksit, the director, and then the younger man with the longish hair—Campari. It was Campari who arrived carrying an armload of what seemed to be plans and blueprints.

A few minutes later a truck pulled up and parked near the foundation site. Two men got out and started to set out small wooden surveyor's pegs . . . foundation work.

Didi placed the baited traps in a clump of poplar trees by the riverbank. For the first time she saw a small floating dock and two small boats moored to it.

The caretaker suggested another place for the traps. Didi ignored him and walked to the trailer.

She knocked twice and this time didn't wait for a response before entering.

The director, Arksit, seemed to be perturbed by her swift entry. "Any trouble with our squirrels?" he asked, a bit testily, a bit mockingly.

"Not at all. Everything is going fine. I was just wondering if I could steal a cup of coffee."

"On the house," he said, and pointed to a Mr. Coffee machine in a nearby alcove. Didi poured herself a cup, shook in two packets of brown sugar, and stood by the machine, sipping, watching the three people studying the plans.

They were so engrossed in what they were looking at, they seemed to have forgotten her presence completely.

The woman finally did, and she asked, "Is there anything else you need?"

It was obvious, Didi thought, that they didn't want her there. But that was a bit weird. She had just arrived. They couldn't possibly suspect anything yet. Why treat her like a bumbling pariah?

It was time, she thought. She plunged in: "Yes. I need your help. Not with the rabies investigation. With this!"

She removed from her pocket a folded-up Hudson River map, one of the ones she had found at the kennel.

She shook it open flamboyantly. She laid it down on the narrow table, over the plans they were studying.

"I collect Hudson River maps," she said. "Like this one. Do any of you know where I can obtain some? Old or new. From collectors or dealers or anyone."

They didn't say a word. They didn't look at the map.

Didi continued, "I don't mean for nothing, of course. I'll pay for them."

Again there was no response. Didi felt very

awkward. She started to refold the map, and as she folded she studied the faces of the trio.

Arksit was looking into his coffee.

Babbington was looking at Didi, not into her eyes, but at a point on her neck.

And Campari was pulling at his long hair with one hand and staring out the window of the trailer.

No doubt, she thought, something was wrong with these people, profoundly wrong. The question was—had the simple unfolding of the map unhinged them so that they acted this way?

When she finished folding the map, Arksit said to her, "What a renaissance woman you are. A veterinarian who tracks down the plague. And an ardent devotee of antique maps of great rivers."

Didi couldn't tell whether he was being sarcastic or not. She didn't care. She had bitten the apple and the serpent was rising. These three individuals, alone or corporately, had to have been the focus of her murdered friend's pyromaniacal rage.

She pressed on with her strange baits.

"I am also looking for an old friend of mine whom I lost contact with. She used to be a pupil at Sunyata House. Joan Benedict."

"When was she here?" the woman asked.

"I don't know. Maybe six months ago. Maybe a year ago.

"We've had many Benedicts," Campari noted.

"A thousand!" yelled out Arksit.

"Maybe ten thousand Benedicts," noted the woman humorously.

They were taunting her, playing with her, making fun of her. Didi didn't care. She had trapped them. They had gone for the bait, in a fashion. The name Benedict disturbed them. The map of the Hudson disturbed them—all of them—in some way . . . in different ways. *She* disturbed them most of all.

Dr. Nightingale walked out of the trailer and went to examine the traps. None had been sprung yet.

She stared at the river. Bait? It was time to fish or cut bait. Wasn't it?

Time either to go back to Hillsbrook and forget about her strange kennel finds or dive into the pool called Sunyata House. Because it was obvious that it was from that pool that the shovel that murdered Rose and Bozo and Aretha had emerged.

She looked at the trailer. It was malevolent.

She looked at the old caretaker whose name she had forgotten. He was evil.

She looked at the grim remains of Sunyata

House and she had a demonic sense of glee. Burn, baby, burn.

Then she realized she had to get hold of herself. She got into her red Jeep and drove to Raymond Buckle's.

When she arrived she was in a strange fury. Buckle was on his porch drinking milk from a container. He was wearing a pair of old-fashioned pajamas—faded flannel like Didi's faded flannel shirt, so thin from repeated washings it was a summer garment.

Didi realized it was only eight o'clock in the morning.

Buckle's face contorted into a smile when he saw her.

"Do you want some breakfast?"

"No," she said. "I want you to tell me about those three people who run Sunyata House."

"I already told you what I know. Did you get to that kennel? The Hanly place?"

"Yes."

"And?"

"Yes. She kept the dogs there."

He nodded. He said nothing else.

She sat down on the step. He drank more of the milk. For some reason she always felt comfortable around grown men who drank milk. Had her father drunk milk? She could barely remember what he looked like, much less his food preferences.

From where she sat she could see an ugly cone-shaped hornets' nest, gray and grim, hanging from the roof.

"A penny for your thoughts," he said.

She realized she had been staring—no, glaring off into space.

"I keep thinking about those three people at Sunyata House. The director and his two spiritual cohorts, or whatever they are. I find them malevolent."

"You have it all wrong," he said.

"I don't think so."

"Do you think I'd lie to you about their reputations in Albertsville?"

"I think," Didi replied, "everyone around here lies."

He seemed to flinch at her words, and flush a bit. Then he was silent. Then he sat down on the step beside her, very close, his knees touching hers.

He said quietly, "You're right. I did lie to you about what I know. I lied because you seemed so goddamn vulnerable."

Didi exploded: "Vulnerable? Don't you mean soft? Isn't that what you mean?"

"No."

"Well, listen to me, Officer Buckle—or do I call you former Officer Buckle? Don't patronize me with your idiotic beliefs . . . about me or about the world. I can outrun you, outthink you, outhunt you, outwalk you, and given the fact that you seem to have only one operative arm, I can probably outfight you. Soft? Vulnerable? I'm a vet, you idiot. I've been trampled by an elephant in Asia, kicked by a great-grandson of Northern Dancer in Saratoga, and bitten by a crazed tiger in a traveling circus in Albany, New York."

Didi was astonished at her outburst. At the sarcasm. At the cruelty of her words.

Yes, she thought, this place is poison.

"Okay," he said. "What I know is this. Sonya Loomis was promiscuous as hell. She very quickly developed a reputation for being wild. And she had a raging, passionate on-and-off-again affair with the director of Sunyata House, Arksit."

Didi muttered in response, half-heartedly, "Rose didn't like old men as lovers."

"All I'm telling you is what I heard. I would assume the mix is one-third fact, one-third fantasy and town gossip, and one-third lost in the transmission. Like, if someone asks you a week from now—'So you met Buckle, huh? How disfigured is he?'—the answer you give will be garbled, right? Why? Because you're a scientist, a veterinarian. But you also like me. So you may have a contradictory response. You must have one."

"Are you sure I like you?" Didi asked.

"I get the feeling you do. Maybe I'm just whistling Dixie."

Quickly, without thinking, she kissed him lightly on the face. He stared down. Then he kissed her back quickly, chastely.

She turned, placed a hand on each side of his face, and kissed him passionately on the lips.

Joined like this, they stood.

Joined like this, at the lips, they walked sideways into the house, in a kind of desperate erotic pavane.

Didi felt incredibly lightheaded. And strong. And wild. She felt like she was leaping off a steep cliff into coral waters without the slightest fear.

No words were spoken. They made love half-clothed on the hard, dusty floor.

Ike Badian arrived at the Nightingale place just a few minutes after 10 A.M. He found Charlie out in the barn watching the Corgi, Huck, who had been let out of confinement and was now having a fine old time investigating the cavernous barn, the pigs, and Promise Me, Didi's big thoroughbred horse.

"Why you want to see that woman again?" Ike asked. "Another dream?"

"Nope. Just some clarifications."

Charlie had decided not to confide in his friend concerning his true intention in going out to see Lily Black again—an investigation into the murder of Rose Vigdor. Ike wouldn't understand his passion for a fitting, fond remembrance vis à vis the doc. And he wouldn't understand how Charlie was going about that investigation.

But it was the only logical place to start, because Rose had been at Lily's before she was murdered, and she had to have been there because of a dream. Charlie had consulted one of the three books in his room—a very old anthology called *Omnibus of Crime*—and in it he had found Sherlock Holmes's dictum, which the great detective had enunciated while investigating the theft of a race horse. That dictum was clearly stated to Watson: "'Crime is common, logic is rare. Therefore, it is upon the logic rather than upon the crime which we must concentrate.'"

"I don't want to hang around at Lily Black's place," Ike protested. "That lady gives me the creeps."

"No one's asking you to stay around. Just drop

me off, go into town, and pick me up in a few hours. That's not hard to do."

Ike grumbled, but that meant assent.

The two old farmers stood in silence and watched the Corgi run all over the place.

The big horse was watching the dog also, a bit nervously. Once in a while he snorted and rolled his eyes. Huck then started harassing Sara, Charlie's prized sow, who ignored him. His feelings hurt, the little dog raced back to the horse's stall, stuck his head through a slat, and started to bark.

Promise Me started to paw the ground with his left front hoof.

Charlie felt a sudden twinge of fear and excitement. This, he thought, could be the VD. It could happen in seconds. The big horse could break through the stall and smash him into the ground, splitting his head open like a ripe casaba melon.

It didn't happen. Huck suddenly collapsed onto the ground, panting, then curled up and proceeded to nap. Promise Me calmed down.

Ike pointed to the exhausted Corgi and said, "If he could talk, what a tale he could tell . . . huh, Charlie?"

The two men walked out of the barn. Ike drove him to the widow woman's place and left him at the roadside.

Lily Black was in the small garden at the side of the house, propping up petite tomato plants with twine and sticks. Her dogs did not seem to be around. Her long white hair was loose and she wore a house dress much too big for her with a dazzling bright pattern of black-eyed Susans splattered all over it. She wore no shoes or socks.

When he was some twenty feet away from her, Charlie stopped and waited. She didn't look up. He realized she was not yet aware of his presence.

It was a warm, cloudy morning. There was no breeze at all. There was silence. The stomach problems he had been having all morning—the gastrointestinal curse—had vanished. The painful cramps were gone.

He felt very calm. There was a strange, beautiful smell in the air . . . a kind of dampness. Like he was standing in a cow pasture. But there were no cows on any part of Stan Black's property anymore. Peculiar, it was, that smell, as if a beautiful past had suddenly reared up and bitten him gently.

Perhaps, he thought, this is what happens just before a violent demise.

"Hello," he called out.

Lily stood up quickly, obviously frightened, then composed herself and said, "I'm sorry. I didn't know you were standing there. I didn't hear a car drive up."

"Ike Badian dropped me off by the road."

"Well, it's nice of you to visit me again."

"I thought maybe you could tell me something about that girl."

"What girl?"

"You know. The envelope. Rose Vigdor."

"What a strange coincidence, Charlie. There were two men here last night, asking all kinds of questions about her."

"A state trooper?"

"I think one of them was. But he wore regular clothes. And the other one was that policeman from town—Officer Voegler."

She returned to her plants, adding, "I will have coffee for you shortly. Or milk and shortbread cookies."

Charlie felt awkward. "What did you tell them?"

She cocked her head and smiled. "I told them the truth. Why wouldn't I? She knocked on my door. I didn't know her, except I had seen her in the village a few times. When she knocked on my door she just made small talk. She asked me a few things. Like did I know a good seamstress in Hillsbrook. Things like that. Then she asked me for that favor."

"You mean the letter?"

"Yes. The two men wanted me to tell them what was in the envelope. I told them I didn't know then and I don't know now. But I do think the reason she stopped by was to give me that letter to mail in case something happened to her. They told me so far they had found no one who had seen her in Hillsbrook except me, a gas station attendant, and a fellow with one of those morning coffee vans that sell donuts off the highway. And most of those people are outside of Hillsbrook. They told me she probably picked me out because I don't know anyone in her social circle. So I couldn't report she was in Hillsbrook. I asked them why she would hide the fact she was in Hillsbrook. They said they didn't know."

Lily returned to the tomato plants.

Charlie wished that the doc had given him some inkling as to what was in the letter he had delivered to her before she ran off to God knows where in order to recover. But she had said not a word. Too bad . . . the contents would have been invaluable to his investigation.

He said to Lily, "You know, I haven't had that dream again."

"That's good, Charlie."

"But it doesn't matter, does it?"

She looked at him sadly, tenderly. "It usually doesn't, Charlie. Dreams are messages."

"From who?" was his angry response. He was shaken by the way she had looked and spoken to him—obvious compassion toward a dead man. She didn't answer. Charlie realized that he had been weak and stupid to go over the truth of her reading of his dream once again. He was there on business. He was there because he had totally accepted her reading of violent demise; and he was there to ensure a fond remembrance. Wasn't he?

"Did you tell them about the dream?" he asked.

"You mean the policemen? Don't be silly. Of course I didn't. Your name didn't come up at all. Besides, your dreams are none of their business."

"I mean Rose Vigdor's dream."

"I don't know about her dreams. I told you what we talked about when she suddenly showed up out of the blue."

"I was sure, Lily, that she came to you with a dream. I thought maybe, out of professional courtesy, like a priest, you couldn't disclose that fact."

"You're wrong, Charlie. She never mentioned a dream when she was in my house."

Charlie nodded, but he didn't believe her. He believed she was telling him a bald-faced lie. He didn't know why, except she might consider it privileged information. She was hiding Vigdor's dream of violent demise. And in that dream had to lie the solution of the triple murder—Rose, Bozo, Aretha.

He evaluated the situation. The path was clear. The logic was excruciatingly clear. He would have to obtain her confidence. He would have to insinuate himself into her life, intimately, quickly—because time was short.

"I would love some milk and shortbread cookies," he said.

"In a moment, Charlie. In a moment."

Dr. Nightingale sat on the bed in her motel bungalow. The clock read forty minutes past one in the afternoon. She felt dazed, ashamed of herself, and borderline suicidal.

She knew what had happened. She'd had wild sex with a total stranger on a floor.

She didn't know how it happened. She couldn't recall or recount the steps leading up to the seduction. Seduction? Who had seduced whom?

The whys were the only things she could dimly grapple with.

An act of vengeance against Allie Voegler? Against Rose?

The act of a woman who had temporarily lost her mind due to the stress caused by a friend's murder, a lover's betrayal, severe financial difficulties in her professional life?

Yes! Plead temporary insanity!

She burst out laughing and brought her legs into the lotus position on the bed. The idea that she was pleading temporary insanity to the charge of bizarre sexual promiscuity was truly laughable.

But the mirth did not last long. The hollowness returned. And the sense that Albertsville was a malevolent place.

She reached into her bag and came up with two pears she had purchased from a roadside stand. She ate them slowly. The phone rang intermittently. Didi knew who it was—Raymond Buckle. She had nothing to say to him.

After discarding the pear cores, Didi took a very long shower, then drove over to Sunyata House to inspect her traps.

There was one squirrel in one trap. A big old dull gray buck squirrel with a long, thin tail.

Dr. Nightingale squatted beside the trap. "You should be ashamed of yourself," she said to him. "A smart old boy like you getting suckered like this for store-bought peanut butter and crackers."

The squirrel did not seem perturbed by the insult. He did not even seem perturbed by the trap. Maybe he had done time in Havaharts before and knew they were country club traps, designed for soft landings and quick releases.

Didi then began an elaborate mime play in which she held up syringes, closed and open the lids of small bottles, put on and took off sanitary gloves, and jotted down nonsense remarks in a notebook.

When she had finished the mime show, she opened the trap and the squirrel scooted free.

And then she looked around to see if anyone had caught her show.

Indeed they had!

Standing in front of the trailer was the handyman, the woman instructor, Babbington, and the director of Sunyata House.

Dr. Nightingale waved to them. None of them waved back. Even at that distance, Didi could sense enmity in their glances. She brought her hand down quickly. They probably knew, she thought, that she was not there to vet squirrels for rabies. They probably knew from the first moment she had stepped onto the property.

She threw her veterinary props back into the satchel. Her eyes caught what only could be called Rose Vigdor's legacy, lying in the satchel haphazardly, the envelope with the $22,000 check she could not or would not deal with yet. And there was the sheaf of Hudson River maps which seemed to mean nothing to everyone. And there was the sheaf of strange envelopes sent to Rose from a Joan Benedict, who lived in Manhattan on West 110th Street, a street that Didi knew was very close to Columbia University, if that meant anything. Yes, it was a festering satchel.

The trio at the trailer was still looking at her. Didi, feeling angry and spiteful again, waved and smiled.

This time the caretaker raised his right hand in a tentative response.

She snapped her bag shut and returned to the Jeep. She realized she had forgotten to rebait the trap. So what?

She started the engine. They kept watching her from the front of the trailer. She gunned the engine but didn't shift gears.

She had to go somewhere, but she had nowhere to go.

Back to the motel?

Back to Hillsbrook?

Back to Raymond Buckle?

No, she didn't want to go to any of those places or people. She should call home, she thought, even if she didn't go home. What about her practice? But the idea of talking to Mrs. Tunney or any of her elves was unbearable.

Dr. Nightingale leaned over the wheel, suddenly dizzy. Then she jerked her head back. The dizziness was gone. She flicked on a tape, a very old one she had found at a church sale in Philly when she was going to school there—Julie London singing "Cry Me a River."

Chapter 7

They were standing in the kitchen when Charlie heard Ike's horn. He looked out the window and saw the pickup waiting by the road, where the drop-off had been.

"I have to go," he said to Lily. He was about to add that perhaps he should spend the night, but that was perhaps a bit premature. Maybe a long way premature.

She was cleaning their lunch plates. It had been a wonderful few hours. They had talked about old times . . . about dairy men and women and the lives they had led . . . about Hillsbrook when it was different . . . about Hillsbrook when you couldn't even approach the town without a heady whiff of butterfat.

There had been a lot of laughing, but once, Lily had broken down and cried, and Charlie had gone over to her and held her hand tightly. My, he had thought as he was holding her hand in his—which was an arthritic, discolored claw from mucking out cow barns for sixty years—it had been a hundred years since he had held a woman's hand. But people, he imagined, did strange things before a violent demise, particularly if they knew it was imminent, and he surely did.

"Maybe I could come back tomorrow or the next day," he suggested. "Maybe you could put me to work in the garden."

"That would be nice," she said, but she didn't look at him.

"And maybe you could tell me more about my crazy cow dream," he said.

She answered quickly, quietly, firmly, "There is nothing else to say."

"Or Rose's dream," he threw out casually.

"I already told you, Charlie, she didn't come here with a dream."

"Right. I forgot."

She dried her hands on a towel and walked him to the front door.

She kissed him lightly on the head. Everything this woman did, she did lightly, if that was the right word.

Charlie thought: I have become one of those movie private investigators. I fall in love with the femme fatale I am investigating. Like in *Chinatown*. Like in *The Maltese Falcon*.

The trouble was, Charlie could not be sure if this was really love or if she was really a cocoon of loveliness hiding a butterfly of evil. He almost blushed for his opulent thoughts.

Of course she was lying about Rose Vigdor—that he knew. The state trooper didn't know it. Voegler didn't know it. But he knew that she had to be lying. It was supremely logical.

He trudged slowly back to his friend's vehicle. Ike seemed to have fallen asleep at the wheel.

Charlie needed a nap also. This detective stuff was exhausting. But what he needed even more than rest was a trigger that would open all the doors fast.

He climbed in beside Ike, who didn't wake up. Charlie leaned over and honked the horn. That did it. Charlie looked back at the house. Lily was outside now with her terriers. She seemed to be making some kind of gesture. Ike started the engine. Charlie squinted toward the house. Yes, my God, there was no question about it—she was blowing him a kiss. He felt very peculiar.

She was driving fast, for her—fifteen miles over the limit. The wind was whipping her face.

And Patsy Cline, who had replaced Julie London, was singing loud.

Only when she passed the turnoff which would have taken her home to Hillsbrook without a wink . . . only then did she know where she was headed.

She was going to New York City to visit Rose's pen pal during those last days—Joan Benedict.

Didi questioned her own motives.

Was it really to discover the contents of those strange envelopes? Or was it to find a new friend to substitute for a dead friend?

After all, Rose had been important to her. Rose was hip. Rose was cool. Rose knew which music was good . . . which books . . . which fashion.

Didi went her own way, but she loved to hear Rose's acerbic monologues about one cultural thing or another, now spoken of course from the perspective of a nature girl.

Dr. Nightingale arrived on West 110th Street in Manhattan late in the afternoon. It was her first visit to the city in three years and she had never been in this particular neighborhood, although she knew Columbia University was only a few blocks north.

She parked the car in a lot on Amsterdam Avenue and entered an old apartment building. It was a well-kept building, but there was no door-man.

The second door was locked, with access only through an intercom.

She pressed 3E, which read J. Benedict. She felt an anticipatory chill . . . as if she knew she had done right coming down here and as if this number 3E could clear up many mysteries.

A voice answered almost immediately. "Yes?"

"Joan Benedict?"

"Yes. Who is this?"

"My name is Deirdre Nightingale. I'm a friend of Rose Vigdor's from Hillsbrook."

"I don't know any Rose Vigdor. I don't know you."

"Wait! Please! It's important. I have your let-ters to her. I know you wrote to Rose in Al-bertsville."

The voice on the other end of the intercom be-came brittle and ugly. "Get out of the lobby or I'll call the police."

Didi responded with a *cri de coeur.* "Rose is dead! She's been murdered! I must talk to you!"

She heard the woman take a breath, as if she were swallowing something, and then came a kind of moan . . . a long, distressing moan or wail seemed to come bubbling out of the intercom.

"Are you there? Are you okay? Please let me up."

The buzz came. Didi ran up the stairs. The door to 3E was ajar. She slipped in. A heavy-set middle-aged woman with very thick glasses was seated on the sofa. The woman looked dazed. The apartment was huge and filled with paintings and vases and large standing lamps and framed family photographs.

She seemed to have recovered, but she was very pale and her chest was rising and falling too quickly. When she saw Didi she patted the sofa.

Didi sat down.

"Are you really her friend?" Joan Benedict asked.

"Yes."

"Is she really dead? Murdered?"

"Yes."

"You know she came here after she left Hillsbrook? She was tired and disillusioned with her life up there. She told me it had not worked out—her dream . . . with that barn and everything."

Didi winced but said nothing. Joan continued.

"Oh, it wasn't me she came to see. It was my son Ivan. They had worked together on a magazine called *Mode*. But she didn't know that Ivan was dead. You can't find refuge with the dead."

"When did he die, Mrs. Benedict?"

"About a year ago. But Rose didn't know. You see, it happened all so fast. They said it was a freak accident. That's what they said."

Didi began to sense a connection.

"Where did he die?"

"In Albertsville, New York. At a place called Sunyata House, a Zen Buddhist retreat, or so they say. Ivan was a student there. And then suddenly my boy was dead. One moment he was happy and the next moment he was gone. A boating accident, they said."

She suddenly laughed wildly and thrust a small framed photograph at Didi, who took it.

"So when Rose came here, I asked her to help me. I asked her to go to Sunyata House, take the Walking Zen course like Ivan had, and find out what had happened. She was very unhappy. Maybe I took advantage of her unhappiness and her shock at discovering Ivan was dead. Yes, maybe that is what happened."

The woman seemed to be drifting off into personal memories. Dr. Nightingale started questioning her sharply.

"Did you pay her fees there?"

"Yes. I sent her the money each week."

"In cash?"

"Yes."

Didi now understood the sheets of blank paper in each envelope—to wrap the cash in so it would not be detected and stolen in transit.

"How much?"

"One thousand dollars."

"But it cost only seven hundred dollars per week. I read the brochure."

"Rose said she needed an extra three hundred a week after she was up there a while. She needed to rent a garage for her new car."

"Did she find anything out about your son?"

"I don't know. The place was burned down. Rose did it. I assumed she had found out something dreadful but didn't want to tell me."

"You mean Rose burned down the place to in some way avenge your son's death?"

"Maybe. What does it matter now? The same people who killed Ivan killed her."

"She was murdered in Hillsbrook, Mrs. Benedict."

"So?"

"So Hillsbrook is a long way from Albertsville."

She laughed. "You don't understand. They are killers. Have gun, will travel."

"Rose was murdered by a shovel."

"No, Miss Whatever your name is—she was murdered by Nothingness. Like my son. Isn't that right? Isn't that what sunyata means? Nothingness. For some Buddhists, I hear, it is the same as paradise."

She pointed at the photo she had thrust into Didi's hands. "Look at him!" she ordered. "So you'll know that it was their paradise that murdered my son. But listen—Oh, God—the boy so loved that place."

Didi stared at the photo. Two men standing in front of Sunyata House. One had to be Ivan. A burly young man with a great big smile, wearing jeans and a hooded sweatshirt. The other man was one of those visiting saffron-robed Asian monks Didi had seen in the Sunyata House brochure.

"He made friends with everyone there," Joan said. "That was his friend Dak."

"Where is this Dak now?"

"Oh, he went home long before Ivan was murdered. He went back to the Andes."

"Were you in contact with the Albertsville police about the death of your son?"

"Of course. I never stopped calling them. I went up there. I called my senator, my congressman. I wrote letters. I cursed. But the police up there would not budge. They kept claiming it was an accident. They kept claiming they'd investigated thoroughly. They kept saying that all the facts showed that my son was drunk, stole a rowboat, went out onto the river, and drowned. That's why I asked Rose to go there. I never realized it would end like this. I should have known—Dear God in heaven, I should have known."

Didi walked out, confused, heartsick. This "thing"—whatever it was—was continually expanding. Like poisonous maple syrup spilled on a Formica counter. Or more appropriately, it was like one of those rare veterinary nightmares—walking among a herd of sick cows . . . each one erupting with and exhibiting different and conflicting diagnostic symptoms.

She walked woodenly uptown on Broadway. The streets were crowded, hot, noisy. It was night now, but it could have been morning. Usually the streets of Manhattan excited her, charmed her, invigorated her—but now she did not respond at all.

Rose had never mentioned this friend Ivan Benedict to her, but she had mentioned the magazine where they had both worked, *Mode*. It went under.

Dr. Nightingale walked into an air-conditioned restaurant on 112th Street and Broadway. It had a large bar. She sat down and ordered a Bass ale.

The moment she sipped the cold brew, she felt a stab of guilt about leaving Joan Benedict so abruptly, in her misery, alone with all those framed photos. A mother in hell. Was there anything sadder?

She put her cell phone on the bar and stared at it.

Then she called Raymond Buckle.

The moment he heard her voice he started babbling: about how wonderful it had been with her, about how this was the first time he had made love to a woman since his accident, about how astonished he was at his own strength and passion, about how beautiful and different she was and the kind of woman he had never encountered before, about how ashamed and excited he was at the suddenness and impropriety of their lovemaking on the floor.

On and on he went—gasping for breath between thoughts.

She finally interrupted him with: "Please be quiet. I want to ask you a question about Ivan Benedict."

There was an astonished pause on the other end of the line, and then: "How do you know him?"

"I just talked to his mother."

He didn't reply.

"Did you work on the case?" she pressed.

"Yes."

"Mrs. Benedict says her son was murdered."

"She's demented," he replied. "The man died by drowning. The autopsy verified that. He was seen taking the boat alone. He was staggeringly drunk. He fell out of the damn boat. Or it capsized. There was no evidence of anything else. Unless you believe some frogman climbed out of the water in the middle of the Hudson River, pulled him out of the boat, and held him under."

His speaking had now exhausted him. She could hear him trying to recover.

"I have to go," she said. For the first time since the conversation started, she recalled the sex with him. It made her feel like an errant child.

"No! Wait! Please! Talk to me!"

She hung up and placed the phone back on the bar. She believed what he said about Ivan Benedict. But she was trembling.

Fifteen minutes later she called Allie Voegler in Hillsbrook—with trepidation.

But the moment she heard his calm, studied response to her voice, she knew he was playing one of his games and this one was fine. He would be formal, polite, proper, disinterested.

"How have you been?" he asked.

"Fine. And you?"

"Okay. Seeing the country?"

"Sort of. Tell me, Allie, did you and Mikoyan find the car?"

"What are you talking about?"

"Rose's car. Was it found?"

"Of course. Not far from where she and the dogs were murdered."

"Was it the old green Volvo?"

"Yeah."

"Did you find anything in it?"

"Just junk. No prints other than hers. No leads."

"What about garage receipts or something like that?"

"No. Why should anyone put that heap in a garage?"

There was silence. The tension was beginning to rise. She could feel it.

"When are you coming back, Didi? I think we have a few things to say to each other."

"Nothing to say. Nothing to explore. Nothing to mull over." She hung up. She felt bad instantly. She should have thanked him.

The bar was beginning to fill up.

What had she learned?

That Rose coaxed $300 a week extra from Joan Benedict to garage a new car in Albertsville—but she didn't have a new car.

That Rose had played private investigator into a murder that most likely was no murder at all.

That Rose had had some kind of intimate relationship with Ivan Benedict.

That Rose Vigdor a.k.a. Sonya Loomis probably did not arrive at or leave from Sunyata House for any reasons pertaining to spiritual enlightenment.

So what?

Now I truly must go home for a while, she thought.

Dr. Nightingale left a third of the ale untouched, exited the bar, retrieved her Jeep, and headed back north toward Hillsbrook, driving slowly, very slowly, because she was so weary.

It was late for Charlie to be up, past 10 P.M., but he couldn't sleep. He sat in the kitchen and sipped apple juice in the dark.

He stared out the window. His VD, he realized morosely, could come in twenty seconds or twenty minutes or twenty days. It was with him all the time. It could come through the window on a dark summer night like this one—a gunshot, a tree limb, anything.

He pulled his eyes away from the window. Keep your eye on the ball, Charlie, he thought.

Think of Lily, he thought, who would talk intimately to him soon, and tell him secrets and tell him Rose Vigdor's dream.

Think of Doc, wandering God knew where now, in mourning for her dead friend. She would remember him fondly, quite soon. She would remember him as the friend she never really acknowledged, as the person in Hillsbrook she really could trust, as the old amateur who solved the crime that had baffled the professionals.

Charlie heard footsteps.

Mrs. Tunney? He groaned. He could not bear Mrs. Tunney now. But no—it was only Trent Tucker, a bit tipsy from his usual ration of two beers at the roadside bar where the disaffected young of Hillsbrook hung out.

Trent flicked on the light, said, "Hi, Pops," and went to the refrigerator.

Charlie bristled. He hated it when the boy called him Pops.

"You drinking with your out-of-work buddies again?" he asked the boy nastily.

"Right. You got any other suggestions?" Trent Tucker retorted. He grabbed some cold meatloaf on a plate from the refrigerator and brought it to the table.

Charlie felt a sudden urge to talk to the boy.

"Is it good?" he asked, pointing to the cold meat.

"Hell," replied Trent, upending the Heinz bottle, "if you put enough ketchup on anything, it's good." Then he took a big bite, chewed it, and added: "A good meatloaf is like a good woman."

"That's a stupid thing to say," Charlie said.

"Well, Pops," Trent replied, his tipsiness becoming evident, "you don't know anything about women anymore."

"And you do?"

"A bit," Trent Tucker replied with a hint of braggadocio.

Charlie bent over and folded his arms on the table. He felt his juices rising.

"Yeah," he said laconically, "I forget that you used to be a ladies' man, at least during the one time during your life you ever had a job, boy."

"Maybe."

"Yeah, I remember that Rose Vigdor thought you were cute."

"Did she?"

"Tell me, hotshot, you ever sleep with her?"

"Are you kidding?"

"Did you ever do anything with her?"

"Nope."

"Would you tell me if you did?"

"Sure, Pops. The lady is dead."

"But you went out drinking with her?"

"Nope."

"You're a lying little creep."

"Now, now, Pops, calm down. I'll tell your nurse."

"I remember you did work around her barn for her."

"So what? That's not a date."

"You know stuff about her . . . don't you?"

"No."

"Sure you do. All your friends down at the bar know a lot about the ladies in Hillsbrook. Isn't that the truth?"

"You're talking stupid, Pops."

"You're gonna give me the information I need, Trent."

"Are you crazy? What information? Let me eat in peace. I don't know what the hell you're talking about."

"I forgot, maybe you're too stupid to understand English. Didn't they boot you out of high school in the second year? Is that it? English ain't your native tongue?"

Charlie was shouting his insults now.

Trent shouted back: "And maybe it's time you went into a nursing home."

Charlie picked up the ketchup bottle by the neck and swung it.

Trent Tucker upended his chair trying to avoid the blow. The bottle missed his head by inches.

He got off the floor and started screaming: "You're a crazy old man." Again and again.

Mrs. Tunney and Abigail rushed in.

"What is going on here?"

Charlie sat back down, letting the ketchup bottle roll along the table. He felt shaken . . . shamed . . . like the king of fools.

His whole body was aching and trembling. He stared at the ketchup bottle.

He knew exactly what was going on. He was trying desperately to implicate Trent Tucker in Rose Vigdor's murder.

He knew he would try to implicate anyone in order to clear Lily Black of any involvement. Charlie lay his face down on the table. He ignored Mrs. Tunney. This love thing, he thought, is nasty business.

Chapter 8

The Taconic Parkway was a beautiful, narrow, twisty four-lane road—very old as highways go. No commercial vehicles were allowed.

At night the road was dark and dangerous even for the wide-awake driver. Didi was no longer alert. She was falling asleep at the wheel and she knew it. In addition, a soft rain was beginning to fall and she had forgotten to put the roof over the Jeep.

She pulled into one of the rest stops—a narrow island off the shoulder which contained gas pumps, bathrooms, and a bank of vending machines for coffee, soda, sandwiches, and candy.

She rolled the top onto the Jeep, filled the tank, locked the doors, and tried to take a quick nap. No use. She purchased some coffee. It was terrible, but she drank it down and then had another one and a ham and cheese sandwich from the machine and a can of ginger ale.

Didi felt a bit better.

On the road again, her thoughts went to that poor woman, Joan Benedict, and her dead son Ivan.

She wondered if he was gay. She wondered if he was not gay and one of Rose's secret lovers.

Didi liked the way Ivan had looked in the photo . . . the easy way he had stood next to that monk from a faraway land.

But that, of course, was really what made Buddhism special, Didi recalled. The Buddhists did not recognize any significance at all in race, gender, class, nation, appearance, talent. Everything and everyone was brought down to either the lowest or highest common denominator—birth, craving, suffering, death.

She smiled as she remembered Joan Benedict's humorous error—that the monk in the photo with her son had gone back home to *the Andes*. A Buddhist monk in the Andes?

Joan must have confused her mountain ranges—she probably meant the Himalayas.

Suddenly Didi was accosted by a very bizarre thought. So bizarre was it that she immediately pulled off the highway onto a shoulder.

What if the term had been garbled in the transmission? Or rather . . . a preposition added? What if this monk—what was his name? . . . Dak—had gone to Andes, a beautiful, peaceful dairy-farming community in Delaware County, easily accessible from Sunyata House?

What if Ivan had told his mother that Dak went to Andes and Joan Benedict did not know the town, or just thought he meant the Andes, the South American mountain range?

Was it possible?

She sat there and thought.

No, she concluded, this line of reasoning was nonsense.

She left the Jeep, stretched her legs for a few minutes, and then headed back on the road.

Twenty-one miles later, when the next rest stop appeared, she turned off again and stopped.

A Buddhist monk who goes to the town of Andes, in Delaware County, New York? Why? How? To minister to the bovines? They are Buddhists by nature.

Or did he simply want to milk a cow before his visa expired?

Was he still in Andes?

Of course not. But if he had really gone there, well . . .

It would be crazy for me to go to Andes, Didi thought.

It would be the wildest of goose chases.

It would be pathetic.

Was she having a nervous breakdown? Was she trying to fly on the most gossamer of wings?

She sank behind the wheel. The dead seemed to wash over her. Her mother. The dog she had loved as a child. Her professor at Penn—Bechtold. All dead now. And Rose.

Didi started to cry, a kind of stubborn diffusion of tears. She kept turning the ignition on and off.

It was getting on midnight.

She wanted to go to Andes. She would go there. Was it because she didn't want to go home?

Dr. Nightingale pulled out of the service area, drove to the Kingston Bridge, crossed to the other side of the Hudson, and pointed her Jeep due west on Route 28 toward the hamlet of Andes.

She reached her destination at two in the morning and spent the night in the Jeep, behind a shuttered roadside store.

At dawn she stepped out of her Jeep and stared in wonder, as she always did in this area, at the bucolic beauty of the land.

There were freshly painted barns and storage silos and herds of milk cows. The hills rolled gently up away from the road, higher and higher, covered with lush grass, until they vanished in the mountains.

The town itself was a half mile north of the highway. She drove there, found a small coffee shop, ate a huge breakfast, cleaned up in the ladies' room, and then called the only person she knew in the immediate area—a veterinarian named Jack Bonsalle.

He was delighted to hear from her. But no, he knew no one in the area named Dak, or any Asian Buddhist monk whatsoever.

He did know of a Cambodian man who had arrived in Andes a few months back, someone named Mr. Nug. At least everyone called him that. Nug made a living hauling trash.

"Could you take me to him?" Didi asked, figuring that this Nug would surely know a Buddhist monk if he lived in or passed through the area.

"What's this about?" Bonsalle asked.

"It's difficult to explain. Let me put it this way. He has some important information that I simply must have."

"Do you want to come out on rounds with me first?"

"I'd love to, Jack, but I'm in a bit of a hurry. Can you get me to this Mr. Nug now?"

He was at the coffee shop in five minutes. They

talked about their profession as they drove in his
new Land Rover.

"When was the last time we ran into each
other, Didi? A year ago, right? At the convention
in Washington. You look different." He laughed.
"Better, believe me. But different."

"I am different," was all she said in response.

They pulled off the road and onto a gravel
path. The Land Rover crushed the tiny stones
like a tank.

Mr. Nug's house was nothing more than a
country shack, but it was well kept, almost pris-
tine.

"There he is," Jack said, pointing to the side
of the house where a short, very thin man in
work clothes was fixing some kind of hose. He
was wearing a silly-looking straw hat.

Bonsalle walked quickly toward him, Didi following.

Mr. Nug saw them, removed his hat, and
smiled.

Jack introduced them.

Mr. Nug stepped forward and extended his
hand stiffly, as if this greeting was in lieu of a
bow.

Didi stepped back away from him quickly and
involuntarily brought her hand to her mouth in
some kind of astonishment.

"What's the matter, Didi?" Bonsalle asked, embarrassed.

"You're Dak!" she burst out accusingly, angry at the man's bald-faced masquerade as a garbage collector.

"No, miss," he said pleasantly. "I am Nug." And he bowed ever so slightly.

Didi exploded. "You're a damn liar. I saw your photo less than twelve hours ago. I held it in my hand. You're one of the Buddhist monks who visited Sunyata House."

Still pleasant, he replied, "No, miss. I pick up garbage. I am Nug."

Didi moved toward him, pointing a finger threateningly.

Jack Bonsalle stepped between them.

"Please, Didi," he whispered, "get hold of yourself. What's the matter with you?"

The three figures stood frozen in silence.

She stared at Mr. Nug's straw hat, which he held lightly in one hand, swinging it like a fan.

Then, without another word, Didi walked back to the Land Rover and climbed in.

Bonsalle drove her back to the coffee shop. He kept asking her what was going on, who this Dak was, why she thought this Dak was Mr. Nug.

She didn't answer. When he dropped her off,

she thanked him and pointed her Jeep toward Albertsville.

Mikoyan was picking at his scrambled eggs in the Hillsbrook Diner, which was crowded with its usual assortment of summer breakfasters—village shopkeepers, tourists out for antiques or roadside fruit and vegetable stands, county road workers, and one or two of the last six real dairy farmers in the area.

Allie, in the booth across from the state trooper homicide detective, was not eating at all, just having some coffee.

It was too early for him. He didn't want to be there. And the less contact he had with Mikoyan, the better.

"I contacted everyone on your list," Mikoyan said. "Nada. No one saw her. No one saw her car. No one saw her dogs. The only witness to Rose Vigdor's presence in Hillsbrook before her murder was that dotty old lady, Black, and she can't give us an exact date as to when Vigdor showed up at her door."

Mikoyan waited for Voegler to respond. There was no response.

He continued, "I also showed Rose's photo to the shopkeepers here in Hillsbrook and in the mall outside the town. Nada."

"She had to eat."

"Damn right. Even if you're hiding in Hillsbrook, you have to eat and drink and bathe." Mikoyan dropped his fork in disgust.

"The real problem," he said to Allie, "is the goddamn time line. We know she torched that place in Albertsville two months ago. We know she was murdered in Hillsbrook a month ago. What was she doing during those thirty days or so? And where? In Hillsbrook? Maybe. Probably. But where in Hillsbrook and with who? And how come no one but that Black lady saw her?"

Allie kept staring into his coffee cup.

"Is it possible," Mikoyan asked, "that she was staying at her old place? The old barn? Keeping out of sight during the day, keeping the dogs tied up, camouflaging her vehicle?"

"She couldn't pull that off," Allie said.

Mikoyan started on his scrambled eggs again. When he was finished he pushed the empty plate to the edge of the table and said, "I think you ought to conduct a real live search of the premises."

Allie was startled. "We've already been over her place."

"Yeah, I know. But I mean strip search the freaking place this time. Barns, property, every goddamn thing and goddamn place."

"And you want me personally to do it?"

"If you don't mind," Mikoyan replied, slipping back into his cool persona and speaking with a rather delicate sarcasm.

"Okay. Just tell me what the hell I'm looking for."

"For starters, evidence that she was staying there before she was murdered. And anything else you can find."

Allie's fury at being used as a kind of flunky was dulled by his grunting, silent acknowledgment that such a thorough search should have been conducted immediately after the bodies were found.

"No problem," Allie replied.

"Good. By the way—any word on the whereabouts of the shy Dr. Nightingale?"

"Shy?" Allie asked, laughing while shaking his head to indicate that he had heard nothing.

Didi lay fully clothed on the bed in her ugly reacquired room in the River Motel in Albertsville.

This is my home now, she thought crazily and bitterly. Why not? If the Buddhist monk Dak could become the garbage man Nug and make his home in Andes, I can become anyone and make my home in the motel in Albertsville.

And my profession? Am I still a vet?

No, she mused. I am now the chief inquisitor. I am a master interrogator . . . I am a brilliant sleuth.

At least she'd better become one quickly, because everything was slipping through her fingers.

And then she laughed at her own pretensions and, for lack of a better term, liquidity of personality . . . a kind of fragmenting, like a young doe lost in a strange wood.

She did know one thing—no more pussyfooting around. She must storm Sunyata House, or what was left of it.

The weakest link would be the woman, because, in a sense, she was the only one of the ruling triumvirate who had appeared normal to Didi.

She stared at the ceiling and wondered if everything in this mess was predetermined. If in fact Serena Babbington, who was ostensibly a holy woman and a teacher of Zen meditation, already knew that she would be visited and interrogated by that country vet with a specialty in cows, Dr. Deirdre Quinn Nightingale.

Besides, they did have something in common. Didi had sat in the lotus position every morning for years on the naked earth. Not doing Zen, of course, but simply yogic breathing exercises. But there was a strong connection; everything was connected for Buddhists.

At two in the afternoon she drove to the edge of the Sunyata House property. She watched the new foundation being laid, but her main focus was the command trailer.

At two-thirty, Arksit and Serena Babbington emerged. They chatted on the steps of the trailer. Then the woman got into her car and drove to a nearby shopping center. Didi followed in the Jeep.

Serena Babbington walked into an Office Depot chain store. Didi followed and caught up with her in the aisle with the stacks of legal pads.

"Hello!" she said to the older woman a bit aggressively.

Serena nodded pleasantly and kept studying different kinds of pads, placing the ones she wanted into her shopping cart.

"It is important that I talk to you now."

"Fine," replied Serena. She leaned on the cart and seemed to give Didi her full attention.

Didi confessed: "My name is indeed Dr. Nightingale, but I am not here on any type of rabies study. I am here because the woman who burned down Sunyata House and who was subsequently murdered was my best friend."

"That you misrepresented your visit here is no concern of mine. Only the consequences are. But I am very sorry for your loss."

"Maybe you are. Maybe you aren't."

"I'm not in the murder profession."

"But one of your friends is."

"Please, Dr. Nightingale, you're distraught. You don't seem to understand what we are about here. We are about ending suffering, not bringing it on. We are about ending the cycle of birth, craving, suffering, death."

There was something so consoling about this woman's presence that for a moment, Didi had the desire to flee rather than hurt her feelings. But she pressed on.

"Did you know a Cambodian named Dak?"

"No. But I did know a Laotian monk named Dak. He was here on a visit along with three of his colleagues."

"Where is he now?"

"Back in Laos, I imagine."

"No. He's not. He's living and working under an assumed name and identity in Andes."

"You mean the little village on the west side of the river? On that road that leads out of Kingston?"

"Yes. It's in Delaware County."

"I find that difficult to believe."

"It's true. I just came from there. I confronted him. He denied being Dak."

"What does this matter?"

"Matter? I don't know. But I think it's strange."

"If true, yes, it is strange. I agree."

"I want to know about your colleagues."

"But why?"

"Because the fire that destroyed Sunyata House might have been set as an act of vengeance for the death of a young man who was once up here—Ivan Benedict. And perhaps the murder of the arsonist was an act of revenge for the arson."

"You seem to be a young woman who lives and thinks in terms of violence."

"Please tell me about the Walking Zen teacher, Campari."

"What is there to tell? He's a fine teacher. He is chaste. He is committed. When he is not teaching, he spends his time in the woods or on the river."

"Is Arksit chaste also?" Didi asked sarcastically.

"Tim is another kind of saint, maybe a piratical saint. He is obsessed with bringing the dharma to America, like the brave eighth-century Chinese monks who brought Gautama's message to Japan. Tim has worked hard. There are now four Sunyata Houses in this country. As for his chastity or kindness—I cannot verify them."

"Are *you* chaste? Are *you* kind?" Didi asked.

Serena Babbington smiled her wonderful smile and her eyes positively twinkled. She leaned over the cart and whispered, "Dr. Nightingale, let me assure you, there is no greater sinner in Sunyata House than me. I am one of the ten thousand devils who stoke the fires of karma."

She started to walk away with her cart.

"Wait!" Didi called out urgently. "I have to talk to you about Rose Vigdor. Do you remember her well? Do you remember Sonya Loomis?"

But the teacher of Sitting Zen seemed uninterested in responding to her anymore.

Didi walked out to her Jeep. She drove slowly, aimlessly around Albertsville. That woman Serena Babbington was impressive and believable. So was Raymond Buckle.

But one element in each of their testimonies did not ring true.

Buckle had told her that Rose was in a passionate affair with Arksit.

That just couldn't be. Rose used to babble on about what men she found attractive. She would never be attracted to Arksit. He was too old, too businesslike, too severe. She would not sleep with him willingly.

And Serena had told her that the saintly Campari was chaste and kind.

In Didi's mind the former was questionable. The young man reeked of eros.

Campari was the one to go after, she realized. It had to be him, Rose's teacher. She knew what Rose liked, what fascinated her.

It would be Campari if it was anyone.

She laughed like a manic schoolgirl. Campari was for Rose.

And who was for her? Raymond Buckle?

She stopped laughing and grabbed the wheel tightly to concentrate on the road. Would she have sex with Buckle again? Did she want to?

Well, if she did, it would have to be less primitive than the first time.

What did she feel for him? It was a strange, anomalous mixture—compassion, desire, aversion.

She was, she realized, beginning to intellectualize to the point of nonsense.

The only thing about the whole incident that she could recall with any precision was the hardness of the floor, the suddenness, the brevity of the sex itself, although even in its brevity it was rather wonderful—and the fact that afterward, she had made a feeble effort to comb his hair.

She kept her eyes on the road. At this point, she realized, there was no doubt that she belonged in the motel, alone.

Chapter 9

Again they were sitting in the kitchen. Lily, at the table, was peeling hard-boiled eggs.

Charlie sat on a stool by the sink, a few feet from her. The windows were wide open and horseflies were zooming in and out.

He loved to watch Lily work at anything. She was always busy in the kitchen or the garden, and when not busy, she was lying down on the beat-up old sofa or on the narrow bed in the tiny bedroom. She would take quick naps, like a cat, and then set about working again.

He watched her remove the shells and carefully stow them in a coffee can. He loved to watch her hands move; her fingers were long and thin and strong.

When he watched her prop up tomato plants or peel eggs or hang up clothes, he felt what could only be called a sexual yearning . . . a desire to do something together with her . . . what, he didn't know.

But whenever they kissed—and he had kissed her several times, once on her naked neck—the sex had just drained out and they were like cousins meeting in a church.

Lily looked up from her peeling, smiled, and said, "A penny for your thoughts."

She always used that phrase, but this time it seemed to energize him. He stepped off the stool and took a step toward her.

Lily noticed the change in him. "What?" she asked.

Look how bright her eyes are, Charlie thought. I want to pick her up and carry her into the bedroom and ravage her.

"Nothing," he replied, and sat back on the stool. "I was just thinking," he said.

"You know, Charlie, I am suddenly very tired."

She got up. "Can you wake me in a half an hour? We can go for a walk."

"I will."

She glided past him, went into the bedroom, and lay down.

Charlie walked into the living room and stared at the reclining figure, easily visible because there was no door to the bedroom. She seemed to have fallen asleep the moment she lay down. He was exhausted from his brief ravishment fantasy.

He stared at the one piece of good furniture in the shack: a huge old maple chest that Lily had probably brought from her old house when she sold off most of the property. Why was he dallying?

Why was he thinking of sex—a man his age—with so little time to live before the VD, and so much still to do?

Did he still believe that the way to Lily's secrets was through erotic intimacy?

He looked at Lily. Yes, no doubt about it, she was fast asleep.

It was definitely time to conduct his search for something that would confirm his theory. It was time to unearth something that would justify and verify his investigation.

And if there was anything, it would be in that chest, for sure.

All Lily's papers and mementos—what there were—were there. He knew that. He had seen her go there to retrieve an old photo of her dairy farm before it was closed down and sectioned off. He opened the chest and began searching, one shelf at a time, moving ever so slowly so that he would not slip and knock something off.

Every few seconds he checked Lily for signs of awakening.

The chest's wood was well cared for. One entered it through swing-out doors with brass hinges and handles. The top part was shelves, the bottom part, drawers.

And Lily was fastidious; everything was piled or placed carefully.

One shelf had legal papers and documents like birth and death certificates and bills of sale.

One of the shelves had photographs and letters.

One of the drawers had old linen doilies and her husband's handkerchiefs, carefully ironed and folded.

One of the drawers had several old pieces of jewelry; Lily seemed to have liked pearls as a young woman.

As the search proceeded, Charlie became more and more pessimistic, and that was why, when he found the *thing*, in what he thought was just another jewelry drawer, it affected him so powerfully, so grievously.

He was not expecting such a blow.

The *thing* was a pamphlet-sized privately printed poetry book of some thirty-two pages, stapled, with a very plain light green cover. The title was *Derelict Orchards*. The author was Burt Conyers.

On the inside front cover was an inscription: "For Lily, who has made my nights like a well of sweet moss."

Charlie replaced the book. He was white as a sheet.

It has happened, he thought. The worst of all possible investigative scenarios. He had thought he was in control, but she was playing him for a fool . . . in order, no doubt, to please her lover.

And it had to be her lover who murdered Rose Vigdor and the dogs, with Lily's help, with Lily's cover-up.

He walked quickly into the kitchen, ran the tap water until it was cold, and doused his face.

When he had steadied himself . . . when he could think clearly again . . . he knew it was time to fix bayonets.

Wasn't that what Philip Marlowe would do?

Campari did not own a vehicle of any kind. He was probably the only adult in Albertsville and the vicinity—barring felons and paraplegics—who did not. This fact made it easy for Didi to isolate and confront him.

She simply waited for him to leave the trailer, followed him by foot about a mile north along the river, and showed herself when he stopped to rest at an old crumbling stone structure that had once been some kind of mill.

When she appeared, as if out of nowhere, he stared at her wide-eyed.

He looks like a wild dog, she thought, the way his eyes are. But he was handsome, oh so handsome, his limbs lithe and strong, his long hair glistening with sweat.

The walk had tired Didi.

They eyed each other warily from a distance of twenty feet.

It was Campari who spoke first. "Are you lost?" he asked. Then he pointed his finger to the east. "The road," he said, "is only a hundred yards off."

"I think," Didi replied, "it is you who is lost."

He smiled. "Perhaps you are right."

"Do you know who I am?"

"Yes. You told us."

"I didn't really. Not you or Arksit. I am Rose Vigdor's friend."

His eyes registered shock. Good, Didi thought. His shock meant Serena Babbington had not spoken to him about their conversation.

"Look at me, Mr. Campari. Do I look like a fool to you?"

"We are all fools," he replied evenly. He stood ever so gently on the earth, as if he were absolutely at ease—even when astonishment had registered in his eyes.

"People around here talk about Rose and that Arksit. That they were lovers. That it was a passion for both of them. But I was her friend—her best friend, Mr. Campari. I know who loved her here. I know who she loved. Quite simply, you!"

He stared down at the river for what seemed a long time, then he turned back to her and raised his hands as if to calm her. "You are distraught," he said.

The more she was in his presence, the more sure she was that Rose and this man had been together.

She could see Rose applying herself to his "Walking Zen." She could sense how Rose would have acted . . . how she would have become quickly infatuated . . . how she would have moved heaven and earth to have him. That was Rose.

Yes, Didi knew she was right, and now she must flush him.

"You see," she said softly, "I know quite well that you are not a saint. I know you were Rose's lover. I know you are somehow connected to the burning of Sunyata House. And I know that Rose's blood is on your hands. Do you hear me?"

He did not answer.

Didi continued relentlessly. "Aren't you going to go into your act, Mr. Campari? Brother Campari? Most holy Zen monk Campari? Oh, I know the act. I mean, I've read about it. You are going to neither confirm nor deny and all you can offer is your compassion for me and for Rose and for all the sentient beings in the world. After all, we are all caught up in the relentless cycle of birth, craving, and death. You work to release all of us from that cycle . . . don't you? . . . do you? Save your bloody compassion. Not all the Walking Zen . . . not all the Diamond Sutras . . . none of it will negate hard evidence presented in a New York State courthouse."

He said nothing, but Didi caught the flicker of fear at the mention of evidence. Of course she had none.

He walked past her and headed back the way he had come.

She had never seen a man walk with such an elegant lope. Calm, erect—but Didi knew in her heart that he was running.

Indeed, she had flushed him.

Didi returned to Sunyata House by a different route and parked her red Jeep by a clump of trees on the other side of the road.

She could see that Campari was back in the

trailer, but she could see no one else through the windows.

It occurred to her that while the trailer was obviously there for those staff members—namely Arksit, Babbington, and Campari—who had lived in the main house, it might be that Arksit and Babbington slept elsewhere and only came to the trailer for their constant meetings on the rebuilding process.

A thunderstorm hit then, a violent, sudden, deafening, frightening outburst, with lightning that made jagged runs in the sky.

When it was over, the air had cooled quite a bit.

Campari emerged at dusk and this time, Didi noticed, he was careful, observant. He looked around before starting off on his walk. This time he was carrying a small knapsack slung over one shoulder.

Didi left the Jeep and followed him. What I lack in surveillance technique, she thought, I will make up in raw persistence.

He was not walking to the river this time, but into town along the main road.

Didi stayed well back, but there was no danger of losing him on this kind of road.

Campari strolled through the center of Albertsville, greeting a few people, not with words but with a slight wave of the hand. Like the Pope waves to the faithful in Rome, she thought.

He turned south at the hair cutter's and picked up his pace.

Now he was on an old road that had fallen into disrepair. As he left the village further and further behind, the shrubs on the road became thicker until it was virtually impossible to tell that the road had once been an active thoroughfare.

A building loomed up. It was one of those ugly low-lying cement-block buildings that usually house light manufacturing firms.

The windows were either painted over or knocked out and the space covered with rusty iron screens. It seemed to be totally abandoned.

The property had become a dumping ground for garbage—all kinds of refuse was scattered around the building.

Campari opened the padlock on the front door with some difficulty and stepped inside.

Didi moved around the side of the building until she came to a screened window, and stared inside.

The space was much larger than it looked from outside. The center of the room was empty, but along the walls were a great many objects that she could not make out.

The thought came to Didi: Was this the space for which Rose had obtained additional money from Joan Benedict? The so-called garage she had rented for the so-called new car she had bought?

Campari, inside, pulled the string of an overhead light. It gave off an eerie glow. He stood in the center of the space and began to empty his knapsack onto the floor.

It took a while before she could identify what he was unpacking. They were face masks that were used for scuba diving and the like.

She felt a chill, and it wasn't from the uncommon coolness of the evening after the storm.

Didi remembered the mocking scenario Raymond Buckle had offered in response to Joan Benedict's belief that her son had been murdered, rather than having drowned accidently while under the influence.

Buckle had quipped that maybe Ivan Benedict was attacked by frogmen in the middle of the Hudson River.

Had the joke become real?

No. No. It couldn't be. She saw no wet suits. Frogmen needed sophisticated wet suits and equipment. These goggles were the kind kids used to peer down when floating on top of the water.

Campari vanished from view. When he came back he was lugging acetylene torches.

He dumped the torches onto the goggles. It looked like he was making a pile in the center of the space.

An altar? A bonfire? An inventory? She didn't know.

With the appearance of the acetylene torches, the goggles made more sense.

Then Campari vanished from sight again.

She heard a bizarre sound.

It was the sound of an engine starting.

Campari came back into view driving one of those small motorized backhoes that are used to dig on construction sites.

The scene became weirder and weirder. Campari brought two more backhoes into the center of the warehouse and parked them there. Then he brought other objects from along the wall and dumped them on his bizarre altar—ropes, picks, tarps.

Didi suddenly realized that whatever this fool was doing, it had nothing to do with anything she had to know about.

Maybe he was cutting himself in for some money from the subcontractors on the rebuilding of Sunyata House.

Whatever the hustle this "saint" was involved

in, one thing was clear: Her choo choo train of investigation had been derailed.

And the trestle that should have carried the evidentiary chain had collapsed into a mud pool.

She turned and trudged back to her Jeep, still parked across the road from Sunyata House. The rain was long over; she took down the top. All she could think of now was the motel and blessed sleep.

Hillsbrook's only plainclothes detective, Albert Voegler, entered the wooded side of Rose Vigdor's property and began to work his way toward the barn. There was about an hour of daylight remaining, and that, he reasoned, would be enough.

He was following Mikoyan's orders to inspect the property thoroughly, but he had no confidence in the order.

It was an ugly trek. These woods were ugly—shrub trees springing up over abandoned cow pasture . . . second-growth woodlands without the anchoring beauty of elegant hardwood trees.

While Allie had little affection for or knowledge of flora and fauna—except for that relating to the hunting of white-tailed deer and black bear—he did see and know that he was walking in a sea of poison ivy, oak, and sumac.

He was sorry he was not wearing boots. He trudged on, cursing Mikoyan and just about everyone else.

About two hundred yards into the woods he smelled gasoline. Now, that was peculiar. He followed the smell to the north and west and within about ten minutes he came to an ugly trampled piece of ground.

It was littered with gasoline cans, dried dog droppings, and several shallow holes that obviously had held burning embers for cooking.

In addition to the gasoline cans, there was other evidence of a vehicle: ruts and wheel tracks, though most of them had now been obscured by mud. No doubt a vehicle had been driven in and out a few times.

He circumnavigated the site slowly, finding scars on the larger trees. That could indicate the use of a hammock.

Voegler stopped, took a few steps back, and tried to survey the entire scene. Rose and her dogs might well have stayed here without being spotted by anyone.

She had been running and hiding, obviously, and this spot was nearly perfect. The well near the barn would provide water. If she needed something in the barn, she could go there late at night. Yes, she had access to everything, and no one in Hillsbrook would ever know she was around.

Voegler took out his pad and ballpoint and drew a rough map of the property and the location of the site he had found. He also listed essential elements of the site.

Then he headed for the barn.

The situation now called for a thorough search and he commenced such a search, although, for a moment, when he entered the cavernous unfinished space, he was afflicted with longing, remorse, and guilt. For there, on the barn floor, was one of the tattered mats on which Nature Girl and he had done their desperate, pathetic little erotic dance—just that one time.

He proceeded to search every crevice of the barn . . . every shelf . . . every chink in the walls. He even climbed the inner scaffolding and checked the tops of the beams.

When it became dark, he went back to his vehicle and got a flashlight. Then he walked the interior perimeter of the barn, kicking at the wood to ascertain if there were any hollow spaces.

He saved the stove and the well for last.

In fact, he didn't have to deal with the well at all, because deep inside the flue of Rose's woodburning stove he found a leather toiletry case.

He pulled it out triumphantly. He could visualize Rose on the run, desperate to hide something, trying to stuff it anywhere—and deciding upon the stove.

He unzipped the case.

First he found three paperbacks. One, a very old book, short stories by a writer named Terry Southern. The second, a newer book, a how-to about growing organic vegetables on raised beds. The third, a brand-new paperback, a manual on salvaging sunken treasure.

This last one was most amusing. Did Rose think silver galleons from the Spanish Main had sunk in the Hudson River?

Then he found something peculiar. It was one of those clear plastic accordion credit card holders.

He let it drop open. Every slot was filled with small photos, head and shoulders, of Asian men. Some old, some young. Many different nationalities were represented—Vietnamese, Laotian, Cambodian, Indonesian, Chinese—but all Asian.

Voegler found himself thinking that there was something definitely familiar about the grain of the photos.

He removed one from its plastic slot and turned it over.

On the back was stamped "INS."

Now he remembered. These were the kinds of photos the Immigration and Naturalization Service issued to local law enforcement agencies, with a request to apprehend and hold, pursuant to deportation.

The Hillsbrook Pub was crowded. Ike and Charlie stuck out like sore thumbs even though they were hidden at the far end of the bar.

Charlie was already on his third beer. He was silent and morose.

"I thought," Ike said to his friend, "that Mrs. Tunney does not like it when you miss supper."

"She don't!" Charlie snapped. "So what? I already missed it. Let her bellow."

"You know, Charlie, you don't look so good. And you sound even worse."

"Why shouldn't I? You don't know what the hell is happening."

"So tell me."

Charlie was silent.

Ike persisted. "I think you're hanging around too much with that dream lady."

Charlie thrust his face next to Ike's and said in a rather urgent whisper, "I got news for you. I love that dream lady, as you call her. I love Lily. And to make matters worse, I also hate her."

Ike moved a bit away from him, hesitated, then signaled to the bartender for two whiskeys.

"Stop drinking this beer, Charlie. Here's some stuff to get your head clear. You sound in very bad shape. You're not making sense."

When the whiskey came, the former dairy farmers downed the shots quickly.

Charlie did seem jolted into clarity.

"So listen carefully, Ike."

"I'm listening."

"You know what I been doing lately?"

"No."

"Investigating a murder."

"You?"

"Exactly."

"Whose murder?"

"Who do you think? Rose Vigdor's."

"You must be kidding."

"You ain't ever seen me more serious, Ike. In fact, I just about solved it."

"Yeah?"

"Yeah."

"Okay. Who killed her?"

"Burt Conyers."

"That's stupid."

"Burt Conyers murdered Rose Vigdor with the help, voluntary or forced, of Lily Black, I am sad to say."

"You sure of this, Charlie?"

"As sure as God made black and white cows."

"Did you go to the cops yet?"

"No."

"Why not?"

"I don't have the smoking gun. You know what I mean? That one single piece of evidence that blows the case apart."

"I don't understand how you did all this investigating, Charlie. I mean, you been spending all your time at the widow lady's and, to be honest, I don't get why you're investigating at all."

"Like I said, Ike, the lady's involved. As to why I'm doing it, I don't have time to explain."

"You look like you have all the time in the world."

"Hell, no! What do you think I'm doing here?"

"Here? Looks like you're drinking."

"That's what it seems like to you. But I'm formulating a plan."

"Tell me, Charlie—why in God's name would Burt Conyers want to hurt Rose?"

"I ain't into motive, Ike. Remember, I'm under a death sentence also."

"Well, good luck on your plan."

Charlie went back to his beer. He seemed lost in thought, his silence occasionally punctuated by mutters and movements of his hands.

Ike dozed at the bar and listened to the juke-box music.

When Charlie drained his fifth beer, his face broke into a large smile and he wrapped one arm around his friend's shoulder.

"I think I have it, Ike."

"That's good."

"But I'm going to need your help."

"Like how?"

"I need one of your old vests."

"Huh?"

"You know, the kind you used to wear to weddings under your jacket. One of those slick reversible silk vests—black on one side and a design on the other side. With the little watch pocket on the side. It was like a river boat gambler's vest."

"If it'll help, Charlie, and if I can find it—you got it."

Chapter 10

The phone sounded like a cowbell.

It woke Didi. She sat up and looked at the luminous dial of her traveling alarm clock.

The clock read 3:40 A.M.

Dazed from being pulled so abruptly from a deep sleep, she grabbed the phone, put it to her ear, but could not speak.

"Didi, it's me. Raymond Buckle. Are you awake?"

When Didi got her voice, she demanded angrily, "Why are you calling me at this hour?" She was used to night calls from panicked animal owners, but she had seen no animals in Buckle's house.

"Calm down. Listen. I would not be calling you if it wasn't urgent. You must get up, get dressed, and get over here now."

"Why? What's going on?"

"Do it! Please! Get over here now!"

He hung up. She slammed the phone back down on the receiver.

Didi sat on the edge of the bed and tried to figure out what was going on.

The air-conditioner was groaning and working improperly. Usually she didn't use air-conditioning, but if one kept the windows open in this motel, one was attacked by mosquitoes.

Then she heard fire engines. One at first, and then many, screaming in the night—obviously volunteer companies from surrounding areas. By the sound, they seemed to be heading toward the village itself.

She got up, showered, dressed, and walked out into the night.

There was a glow in the sky. Was that the fire? Probably. It was in the direction of the village.

She headed toward the Jeep slowly. What was up with Buckle?

Was she right in going there? Or had the man flipped? Was it some kind of physical emergency connected with his disability?

Had that one sexual episode turned him into a desperate Romeo?

She put her hand on the door of the Jeep and hesitated. It was a very warm, muggy night. She was glad she had forgotten to put the roof on the Jeep.

But it was not a night for adventure of any kind.

The thought came to her: Was this summons about Rose Vigdor?

Had Buckle awakened in the middle of the night with a bad conscience? Had he realized he must tell her the truth? Tell her what he knew about Rose and Sunyata House?

She climbed in, started the engine, and flicked on the headlight switch.

The large sycamore trees that bordered the motel parking lot were eerily illuminated by the Jeep's beam—particularly the thick, low-hanging, mottled limbs.

Didi put the Jeep in reverse and started to back out.

A shadow from the tree line caught her eye. An owl? She peered through the windshield. Didi loved owls. They were good omens.

Suddenly she slammed on the brakes.

No. Not an owl.

There was some kind of figure in the trees.

She set the emergency brake and stood up in the uncovered vehicle.

A man was swinging from a limb.

There was a rope around his neck.

And he was dead.

The face presented itself.

The color ran out of Didi's face. She sat down. It was Saint Campari.

He had hanged himself in front of Didi's motel.

She seemed to be very calm in the face of the shock. She remembered hearing that Billie Holiday song "Strange Fruit," about a Jim Crow lynching. The song had always upset her so much she could not listen to it all the way through.

But even though the circumstances were different—the swinging man in front of her had obviously committed suicide—she could not help but think of the absolute accuracy of the song. It did indeed appear to Didi that she was watching a piece of strange fruit.

The body was a mere twenty feet from her.

She could cut him down, she thought. But why? Her practiced eye quickly noted the broken neck and drained pallor. The man had been dead for at least an hour.

She called 911 on her cell phone. She reported the suicide. She did not give her name when asked. The operator did not ask whether she knew the name of the corpse.

Then Dr. Nightingale drove slowly to Raymond Buckle's place.

She walked woodenly into the house—the door had been left half open for her.

Buckle was seated.

"There's a fire somewhere," she said.

Then Didi added, as if it were an afterthought, "And Campari hanged himself in front of my motel."

She heard someone say, "Who's Campari?"

It wasn't Buckle.

Allie Voegler was standing near the kitchen.

It was too much.

She slid down onto the floor, her feet refusing any longer to support the weight of her body.

Both men rushed over to her.

"Stay away! Stay away!" she shouted.

They backed off.

Some very strange thoughts were dancing in her head: that these two men had formed a secret society because they had both made love to her, and they were meeting to pass some kind of judgment or punishment on her.

Buckle gave her a cold bottle of beer. She drank half of it in two dehydrated gulps.

She felt better. She stood up and walked tentatively.

"Why are you here?" she asked Voegler.

"Rose hid something in her barn before she was murdered," he said.

"What?"

He handed her the extended string of photos encased in plastic like an accordion.

Didi stared at the faces.

"Who are these people?" she asked.

"They are all people wanted on INS warrants. Do you know what they have to do with Rose?"

"No," Didi replied.

She brought one of the photos close to the light. Then she looked up at Voegler and smiled. "But I know where you can find one of these men right now."

"Are you serious?"

"Quite serious, Officer Voegler," she replied. "And I'll take you to Mr. Dak."

"Is that his name, Dak?"

"Sometimes it's Dak and sometimes it's Nug and sometimes, for all I know, it's Ho Chi Minh."

Didi shut her eyes. She sat down in the rocking chair. She rocked.

"Let me rest a bit," she said to her two ex lovers, "and then we'll go to Dak."

Charlie waited by the road in front of the Nightingale house; he was waiting for Ike, who was late. Not very late—but late enough.

When the old pickup truck finally pulled up, Charlie didn't even wish his friend good morning.

"You got the vest?" he asked.

Ike held up the old monstrosity—triumphantly.

Charlie climbed into the truck and they drove to town.

"Now," Charlie said, "all we have to do is find Burt Conyers."

"That's easy. He's always with old Harland about this time, in the health food store, to get free coffee and whatever else he can hustle up."

Charlie felt much better. He had run across Conyers in Harland Frick's store when he had brought over his manuscript for the old man to read—but he had no idea it was a regular ritual.

"So you just park in front of Harland's store, Ike, and wait for me. I won't be more than ten minutes. This plan is either going to work fast or not at all."

Before leaving the truck, Charlie carefully folded the vest into a small packet and put it in his back pocket. It stuck out like a bandana.

Burt Conyers was in the store that morning, along with Harland Frick and one of Frick's young delivery boys, Simon Abbott.

The moment Charlie walked inside, old Harland asked, "You got more pages for me to read, Charlie?"

"Not today. Actually, I just stopped by to find Burt."

"You found me, pilgrim," the poet said, sipping his free coffee and tugging at his ever-lengthening beard. He was wearing sandals as usual, and his toes were caked with mud.

Charlie refused the proffered cup of coffee and got right to his point.

He pulled the vest out of his pocket and shook it out so all could see its splendors.

"Well," Charlie said, "I found this in my attic closet. It doesn't fit me anymore by a long shot, so I thought of you, Burt. I mean, there's still a couple of weeks of hot weather left and you must be sweltering in that sheepskin vest."

"That's a nice thought, Charlie," said Harland. The young man, Simon, just grinned a stupid grin. Charlie had never really liked the boy—he was large and ungainly and a bit dim-witted, and sometimes he delivered the wrong package to the wrong house, which was very hard to do in a place like Hillsbrook.

Charlie ignored both of them and held the vest out to Burt.

"Wrap it around a three-legged goat," said the poet nastily.

"Oh, come on, Burt," said Harland. "The least you can do is try it on." He took the vest from

Charlie, roughly pulled Burt's funky sheepskin vest off, and helped him on with the new one.

Everyone admired the new Burt Conyers.

Now Charlie had to make his move, because there were two elements to the plan. First to get Burt to try on the vest, to get the fabric against his body. And second, to make sure Burt didn't keep it.

Charlie said to him, "Yeah, that's you, Burt. It's about time you stopped looking like a wino riding the rails. I mean, after all, a lot of people know you're a famous poet. This vest gives you style, even some . . . well . . . respectability."

The old dairy farmer was right on the money; he had pushed the correct button.

Burt ripped the vest off and flung it at Charlie. There was nothing he loathed more than the Hillsbrook respectability that Charlie Gravis and his idiot friends represented.

Fifteen minutes later, Ike, Charlie, and the vest entered the Nightingale barn.

They found the Corgi snoozing at the side of Promise Me's stall. Charlie dropped the vest in front of Huck, then moved away.

The little dog just stared at it for a moment, strolled over to it, sniffed the fabric calmly, and then attacked it with what seemed to be a demented fury.

They watched as he ripped the vest apart.

"It wasn't a bad vest," noted Ike.

"Yeah, too bad it had Burt's smell on it. Well, Ike, now comes the hard part."

"What's that?"

Huck the Corgi was now running up and down the barn with the shreds of the vest in his teeth, occasionally stopping and shaking it like a rat.

"Let the great poet know there's a witness."

"Why?"

"Because then he'll try to eliminate the witness."

"But Huck can't testify, Charlie."

"You gotta remember, Ike, guys like Burt got wild imaginations."

"Charlie, everyone knows a dog is a dog."

"I don't know anything, Ike. I can't afford to know anything. Don't you get it? I'm in the middle of a criminal investigation."

The three of them rode to Andes in Didi's Jeep.

It was a slow, rather pleasant drive that commenced at the break of dawn.

Neither Buckle, who sat in the back, nor Voegler, who sat next to Didi, spoke.

Dr. Nightingale did all the talking. She recounted to them all that had transpired. What she had found in the kennel. What she had heard at Joan Benedict's apartment. What she had said to Serena Babbington and Campari during her conversations with them, and what they had said to her. How she had obtained access to Sunyata House by the rabies ruse. How she had found the place malevolent. How she had found Campari's body swinging from a tree. How she believed that he had committed suicide out of love for Rose and guilt at having somehow, in some way, been responsible for her death. And she told them of the strange backhoes and gear she had seen in the building near Albertsville, the one that Campari had led her to.

They were only fifteen minutes away from Andes when she finished her narrative. Didi, who had spoken quickly and quietly, stared at her companions to judge the impact of her narrative.

Their faces registered nothing.

She wondered if Raymond Buckle knew that Allie and she had been lovers. She wondered if Allie knew that she had made love with Buckle.

When they reached Andes, Didi could not remember how to get to Mr. Nug's house. She got lost three times in the maze of back roads.

Finally, the red Jeep stumbled onto the Nug

property, and there he was, in his straw hat, changing the oil in one of his small garbage trucks, the one with the deep, flat bed.

When he saw them approach, he wiped his hands, smiled, removed his straw hat, and went to meet them.

What happened next happened very fast. Neither Didi nor Raymond Buckle interfered or said a word.

When Mr. Nug was about five feet from them, Allie Voegler flipped open his badge packet, identified himself, and at the same time bent down, removed an ugly .25-caliber Beretta from an ankle holster, bridged the distance between them, and placed the end of the barrel against Nug's forehead.

The man was so petrified his straw hat fluttered to the ground and he stood as stiff as a board, his eyes frantically criss-crossing on the weapon.

"I want to see your papers," Allie said quietly, but in a voice pregnant with threat.

They all walked into the house. Allie moved the gun to the back of Nug's head. The man produced a passport and additional documents.

Allie looked at them for only a second, then he flung them contemptuously across the room.

He pulled out the INS photo and shoved it

against the man's face. "Your name is Sun Dak. You are a Laotian national. There is a warrant issued for your arrest by the INS. You are charged with entering this country illegally, impersonating a religious functionary, obtaining false documents, and conspiring to subvert the laws of the United States."

Allie let the words sink in. The man's terror was not abating, it seemed to be growing. He couldn't stand any longer.

Allie rammed the gun against the man's neck, literally into his neck, and held him up with the other hand.

"Listen to me. You have only two options. You can be deported immediately. Or you can be deported after serving twenty years in a federal prison. Do you understand me?"

Dak didn't answer.

Allie screamed at him, "Do you understand? Yes or no! No or yes!"

"Yes, yes," Dak said in a cracked whisper.

"If you tell me who gave you those false documents, you won't spend a day in an American prison. I will give you ten seconds to reply."

Dak waited five seconds. Then he asked, "May I sit?"

Allie let him sit down. He pulled the gun back.

"Mr. Arksit," Dak said.

"From Sunyata House?"

"Yes. Mr. Arksit from Sunyata House."

Allie gave Buckle the weapon, then took out his cell phone and called Mikoyan.

Didi could hear the words but couldn't make sense of the call—she was too dazzled by the brutality and the success of Allie's approach. She had not anticipated anything like it.

Allie put the phone back into his pocket.

"Mikoyan," he said, "is calling the state trooper barracks near Albertsville. They'll pick Arksit up. Mikoyan will do the interrogation. It'll take him about an hour to get there."

"What do we do now?" Buckle asked, keeping the weapon pointed away from the still-terrified Mr. Nug.

"We wait," Allie said. "Maybe our friend here will make us some tea."

Charlie Gravis entered, once again, the small health food store. It was just past ten in the morning. Harland and Burt were there, having a morning coffee. The delivery boy, Simon, was not around.

"Charlie, my boy, you're getting to be a regular, like Burt here."

"It's your coffee, Harland," Charlie replied.

"Then grab a cup."

173

"I don't have time."

"There is nothing as pathetic as an old man who's in a hurry," noted Burt.

Charlie gave him a little snarl and then ignored him.

"Look, Harland, I need your help."

"Sure."

"Do you remember what treats Rose used to buy her dogs here? I mean, I know she cooked up her own organic mess for her dogs, but I remember that once in a while she would get some tidbits for them from you—at least Doc told me she did."

"You want some for your yard dogs?"

"No. For Huck. The Corgi. Rose's dog. The one that survived the murder. He's staying with me. He's in bad shape. I can't get near him. No one can. But I was spending some time with him and I saw that under his scruff he got a collar, and under his collar is a clump of some kind of fabric."

"So what?"

"Well, I figure he got those strands during the murder. Maybe from the murderer. Maybe that's why he survived—he took a bite out of the killer. Or at least a nip. The cops can tell a whole lot now just from a few strands. They can get fingerprints from it. They can get tissue samples. Hell, they can get a thousand things. But I can't get close to the little fella, so I need something to persuade him that he should love me and let me get that collar off and get it to the cops."

"Makes sense," said Harland, and he walked to the shelf that contained organic milk bones of all sizes for dogs. He studied the boxes for a long time. Charlie took some coffee. Burt hummed "Mack the Knife."

"The way I figure it, Harland," Charlie called out, "is if you can get me the stuff he likes, I'll start feeding him the bones when I get back, and by tomorrow morning he'll be a pussy cat, and I'll get the collar and the fabric over to Allie Voegler."

"Makes sense," agreed Harland again, and kept on looking.

Finally he pulled a single large box off the shelf and brought it to Charlie. "If I remember, this is what she used to get. Not often, but once in a while."

He handed the box to Charlie, who studied it. It was very expensive. The writing on the box claimed that each bone contained all the daily mineral and trace elements required for good health in a mid-sized dog. The bones themselves, the writing claimed, contained high-grade bone meal, soybean, natural flavors, vitamin supplements, and macerated dandelion.

"I'll take it. Thanks, Harland."

Charlie purchased the box of milk bones, finished his coffee, and left.

Ike was waiting for him around the corner. Charlie held up the box triumphantly as he climbed into the pickup truck.

"Now what?" Ike asked.

"The way I see it, Burt has to make his move before tomorrow morning. So he'll come at night. Late. He'll sneak into the barn and do one of two things. He may just check the collar out. Or he may kidnap the dog."

"There's a third option, Charlie, if you're right."

"What is that?"

"Kill the dog."

"Why would he do that?"

"Why not? If you're right, he killed two other dogs. What does a third mean?"

"You got a point, Ike. We'll have to stake out the barn with some weapons. Bring one of your deer rifles. I got an ax."

"What time you want me over?"

"I figure we take up guard duty an hour or

two before midnight. We stay out of sight. We wait until he enters. We wait until he gets really close to Huck. And then—boom—we take the bastard."

"Sounds good, Charlie."

Chapter 11

It was a long, ugly, uncomfortable day in that little shack in Andes. They waited for the call from Mikoyan.

Mr. Nug did indeed make them tea and even made them a bit of food—a rice dish with cut-up scallions, an egg, and some kind of sauce that was hot to the tongue.

Didi dozed from time to time. Allie wandered about the property. Raymond kept going into the bathroom and washing his face.

It grew very hot. Mr. Nug continually fanned himself with his straw hat. Once or twice he mumbled about how his customers would be very unhappy because their garbage was not being picked up.

The call from Mikoyan came at five-thirty. Allie took it. He took out his pad and pen and began to make notes. He did not interrupt what was obviously a Mikoyan monologue.

The phone call did not end until six-twenty.

Allie said, "I'll tell you about it on the way back to Albertsville."

They dropped Mr. Nug off at the local lockup and headed east.

While Didi had done all the talking on the way there, Allie did all the talking on the way back.

He consulted his notes as he spoke.

"Mikoyan says Arksit broke like a rotten light bulb. He admitted the scam. It was simple and ingenious. The illegals were smuggled over the Canadian border. They were met by Arksit, who provided them with the robes and attire of Buddhist monks. Then they motored happily down the Hudson Valley, knowing that no one would question them, and were put up at Sunyata House while bogus documents and passports were created for them under new names. Then they vanished into the countryside. The price they paid for entry, safety, and documentation was $25,000 U.S. dollars. That's per person.

"Arksit justifies the scam on the grounds that he was giving sanctuary to political dissidents at twenty-five grand a pop.

"Here's what Arksit has to say about Sonya Loomis, a.k.a. Rose Vigdor. All he knew about her at first was that she was pretty, enrolled in the Walking Zen program, and constantly asking questions about a young man who was drowned while attending Sunyata House. Then she started to flirt with him. Arksit slept with her three or four times. He broke it off when he found out she was also sleeping with Campari. After he broke it off, she came to him and told him she knew about the illegals. She began to blackmail him. He doesn't know how she found out. He paid for a while—in amounts of five thousand dollars each time she put the screws on. Then he paid no more. She threatened him with exposure. He still refused. She burned down Sunyata House as a result. Arksit says he hated her, but he didn't kill her and he doesn't know who did."

Allie put the notebook down and lit a cigarette. Didi kept her eyes glued on the road. She was waiting for more . . . much more. Allie smoked slowly, relaxing, then flung the butt out of the car and recommenced.

"It gets a whole lot more interesting. But what I'm telling you now Mikoyan did not get from Arksit. He got it himself. Yes, Campari hung himself. Yes, Campari's warehouse contained exactly what Didi said it did. And Campari torched it before he killed himself. Campari, however, was not Campari. His prints say he was Gerald Mattei. He served two years in a Colorado maximum-security prison. He was convicted of eco-terrorism. He and some friends blew up the feeder cables that utility companies use to drain water from the Colorado River. Now, as everyone knows, the draining of water from the Hudson by utility companies is wreaking havoc on the fish stocks. The fingerlings, the baby fish, are sucked in and killed. The breeding cycles are interrupted. Mikoyan believes this Campari was about to do the same thing in the Hudson that he did in the Colorado River. And Rose was his comrade in arms. She used the money she extorted from Arksit to buy the torches and backhoes.

"Did Rose burn down Sunyata House on Campari's instructions? Mikoyan doesn't know. Mikoyan does know that Campari wouldn't murder his comrade and lover. Her death caused him so much grief, he destroyed the equipment that could have realized his dream and then he destroyed himself."

Allie flipped his notebook closed with a dramatic gesture and added, "That's what we got."

Didi asked in a hoarse, desperate tone, "But who murdered Rose and her dogs?"

Allie replied, "Mikoyan thinks it was Arksit, in spite of his denials."

"And what do you think, Allie?"

"I don't know."

"The whole thing sounds unreal . . . weird."

"What's weird?" Allie shot back.

"What Sunyata House seemed to be . . . and what it was."

Charlie Gravis lay on his bed in the small, dark room, fully clothed, his eyes wide open, staring at nothing on the ceiling.

He felt unbelievably calm. This was the culmination. Let the VD come as soon as it was over; he would have his FR. And that was the most that could be expected. Fate was fate. Character was fate. Fate was a frump. He smiled. What the hell was a frump?

In one corner of the room was an ax, wrapped in a flannel shirt. It was old and rusty and the handle was chipped—but it was serviceable.

Hopefully, he would not have to use it, but a little threat always helped.

The plan was set. He would meet Ike at the front of the secondary road that reached the barn the back way, through the field. Burt Conyers would come that way into the trap, Charlie knew; it was the only way to avoid the yard dogs.

At ten-thirty he left the house quietly. Mrs.

Tunney and Abigail were fast asleep. Trent Tucker was God knows where.

Ike was exactly where he was supposed to be, carrying his old lever-action Winchester deer rifle in the crook of his arm.

"Maybe," Ike said, "we ought to reconsider."

Charlie ignored him. Ike always had second thoughts about everything, and then he had third thoughts about the second thoughts, and then everything was okay.

Charlie handed him a piece of aluminum foil.

"Now we each have a piece of foil. So here's what we do, Ike. You'll be up in the loft and I'll be on the other side of the horse stall just below you. The minute one of us thinks the sonofabitch is in the barn—crinkle the foil. It'll make a loud enough noise to signal the other. Remember, all we want to do is catch him in the barn. That's proof enough of intent to get the dog or hurt the dog. You get me?"

"I get you."

They entered the barn. The animals were quiet. Huck had changed his place of abode and was now settled in about ten yards from Sara the sow.

Ike climbed up slowly and settled himself on a bale of hay, his feet on an upturned water bucket.

Charlie sat down with his back against Promise

Me's stall. He had a clear view of the dog and a partially obscured view of the entrance.

As the time passed, Ike became very unhappy. He realized there was a strong possibility that he had once again become suckered into one of Charlie's idiotic schemes.

Well, it wasn't about money this time, like when he started to build a financial empire on the basis of a famous exterminator, which turned out to be a house cat with a morbid affection for field mice. This time might be even worse. With Charlie wheeling and dealing, one always had to keep ducking.

At one A.M. he wondered whether he should just walk down and announce he was leaving.

Then he heard the aluminum foil creaking from downstairs.

Ike stood up.

Then he heard Charlie shouting, "Hey! Hey!"

Ike hobbled down the stairs as fast as he could, taking the safety off his rifle and levering a round into the chamber.

As he climbed down, he started calling out, "I'm coming, Charlie. I'm coming."

When he set his foot on the ground floor—a horrible explosion went off near his face.

The sound and flash and smell of a double-barrel shotgun at close proximity knocked him over.

Then he sat up dumbly, like a baby in a crib, and started firing his weapon at the two dark figures running out of the barn into the night. One was helping the other.

"Charlie! Charlie!" he yelled. "I'm going after them!" And Ike ran, as best he could, after the strangers, out of the barn, down the road, firing sporadically.

Didi slept over one more night at the River Motel in Albertsville. She left in the morning for Hillsbrook. Voegler stayed in Albertsville, with Mikoyan and the continuously interrogated Arksit.

Didi drove fast and carefully, as if she had just awoken from a stupor and realized she had neglected important tasks during that stupor. There was a hint of the coming fall in the air—a kind of crispness—and she felt like a race car driver behind the wheel.

The moment she entered the incorporated village of Hillsbrook, she pulled over to the side of the road and shut the engine off.

It was so good to be back that she had to contemplate the feeling, to savor it. She had no idea how long she had been away. It seemed like months, though it was only days.

Then Didi drove to her house and greeted the yard dogs, who mobbed her.

Disentangling herself, she slipped past the front door and called out to Mrs. Tunney.

No one was in the house. Not Mrs. Tunney. Not Abigail. Not Charlie or Trent. All the elves were gone.

Maybe they were in the barn, she thought. The moment she entered the barn, Promise Me greeted her raucously. She pulled his ears gently. Huck was happy to see her also—running back and forth barking.

But no other people were in the barn.

She called out: "Hello, hello."

No answer. She started to leave when she caught a strange scent.

It seemed to come from the straw bedding that had fallen or been kicked out of the horse's stall. There seemed to be patches of oil or kerosene.

This is dangerous, Didi thought, and she bent down to inspect the substance.

It took her a while to realize that she was inspecting dried human blood. And there was a great deal of it.

* * *

Allie Voegler was about to leave Buckle's house and head back to Hillsbrook when Mikoyan drove up.

They had spent the morning together, questioning Arksit.

"Anything new?" Allie asked.

"A whole lot," replied Mikoyan.

"Well," said Allie, laughing, "you're the boss, you handle it."

Mikoyan ignored his comments. He asked, "Do you know Charlie Gravis?"

"Of course. The old man who works for Didi Nightingale."

"He was shot."

"What?"

"Shot bad, in his barn, at close range, with a shotgun."

"Why, in God's name?"

"It seems the old guy was working the Vigdor case on his own. He came up with a suspect—a crazy poet named Conyers. You know him?"

"Yes, of course I do. And you know him also. At least you talked to him. He was one of the names on the list I gave you."

"Anyway, he set a trap, the old man did. He told this Conyers that the dog who survived the massacre and now lived in his barn had a collar

187

on and the collar contained evidence from the murder—wisps of fabric. This Charlie and his friend Ike staked the place out. They figured Conyers, if he was the killer—and they believed he was—would have to get the pooch. And it went down—boom!"

"You mean Conyers showed up and panicked?"

"No. It gets stranger. It wasn't Conyers who showed up. It was an old man and a young man. This Ike chased them off and thinks he wounded one. Anyway, about five hours later, a young guy brings an old guy into the emergency room at Salem Hills Hospital. The old guy is DOA from a gunshot wound. They try to question his companion. He runs and cracks up his car two miles away. He's taken back to the same hospital with two broken legs. The local cops find a shotgun in the car. It looks like the weapon that got Gravis."

"Are they from Hillsbrook?"

"Yeah. We got preliminary I.D.s. The young guy is Abbott, first name Simon. The old guy is a shopkeeper named Harland Frick."

"Hold on!" Allie shouted. He could not believe what he was hearing. "Look, Frick is even older than Charlie. He can't even see anymore. And he wouldn't hurt a fly."

"Abbot says he drove this Frick to the barn to get the dog—and it was Frick who shot Charlie."

"I think we better get over there," said Allie.

They drove to Salem Hills in Mikoyan's car. Allie identified the corpse first. It was indeed Harland Frick.

Then Mikoyan took him to the younger man, under police guard in a third-floor hospital room. Simon Abbott was awake but sedated. He recognized Allie, who sat down on a chair beside the bed.

Mikoyan moved away from them.

Allie had seen the boy around Hillsbrook for years, working at Frick's store, playing ball, fixing cars. He was a good kid, a quiet kid. His mother worked for a mental health clinic on Route 44. His father used to drive a heating-oil truck. He had a sister who was at SUNY-Albany.

"What happened, Simon?"

"Charlie came after us with an ax. Mr. Frick got scared. He pulled the trigger. And then Mr. Badian came down from the loft and started firing."

"Why did Harland want the dog?"

Simon didn't answer.

"The old man is dead," said Allie.

"I know."

"Did Harland believe Charlie—that the dog had some evidence?"

"Yes."

"Why?"

"Because the dogs were biting."

"You mean at the dump. When Rose was murdered."

"Yes."

"Did Harland kill Rose?"

No answer.

"He couldn't have, Simon. He wasn't strong enough to swing a shovel."

No answer.

"Did you kill her?"

No answer.

"Why, in God's name?"

Then Simon started to speak, very quietly, not looking at Allie, speaking, in a sense, to some invisible person at the side of the bed. In fact, he seemed to be dropping his words over the side.

"I saw Rose living in the woods, behind her barn, about six weeks ago. I told Mr. Frick. He went to see her. He was worried about her. She said she had done a bad thing; she had burned down a school, she was a fugitive. And she said that the director of the school was going to kill her. His name was Arksit and I drove Mr. Frick to see him, to try and get Rose off the hook, to see if the man would maybe not press charges, or allow her to make restitution.

"It got crazy. Arksit wouldn't do a thing to help Rose. He hated her. And he offered Mr. Frick a hundred thousand dollars in cash to kill her. I thought it was a joke. It wasn't. Mr. Frick didn't think it was a joke. He thought for about a half hour. We went for coffee at a place in Albertsville. And then he told me he was going to accept Arksit's offer. Mr. Frick told me this was his last chance to get out of a town and a life he now loathed. Mr. Frick said he was going to die soon and he wanted to die free, with money in his pockets. Out of and far away from Hillsbrook . . . far, far away, maybe up in the Adirondacks.

"And he said I could have twenty thousand dollars if I helped him. I didn't believe it would happen. I didn't think he would go through with it. And I didn't think I would be so crazy as to help him. But I never saw that much cash . . . and I could hold it . . . and stuff it into my pocket . . . and buy any goddamn car I wanted . . . and go where I wanted . . . and it was mine.

"We lured her to the dump. I hit her with the shovel. I killed the dogs. And I buried them all."

And then Simon Abbott smiled, the way kids smile when they are bad.

* * *

It was three days after the barn shootout. Charlie Gravis was still in intensive care, slipping in and out of deranged consciousness.

No visitors were allowed.

The wounds had been primarily to the lower abdomen and there had been massive bleeding.

During those days, Didi had gradually let go of her obsessive attempts to understand Rose Vigdor's behavior during her final months. She realized there were some questions that would never be answered.

She could not even begin to fathom how Rose's killer had turned out to be one of the sweetest old men in Hillsbrook.

Sure, Didi had heard rumors that Harland Frick had a dark side when he was drinking. Sure, she could understand how old-timers would hate the changes that had happened in Hillsbrook.

But to hate enough to murder, even with the incentive of $100,000, was mind-boggling. And to turn that hate on Rose Vigdor was incomprehensible. Yes, Rose had been a newcomer to Hillsbrook—but she was, above all, a preservationist.

After Didi had stopped obsessing about Rose and Harland and the whole damn crew, she had begun to obsess about poor Charlie Gravis, lying in his hospital bed.

She had talked to Ike for hours about Charlie's dream and the predictions by the dream lady.

Now, grooming her horse Promise Me in the barn, the same barn where Charlie had been shot, she felt a weird exhilaration.

After all, the dream predictions had been brilliant. Not 100 percent correct, thank God, but close enough. Charlie almost had his VD—violent demise. And he had surely gotten his fond remembrance—she would always be grateful to him for trapping Rose's killers and the people behind them.

As she brushed, Didi realized how sad it was that after all their years of working together, Charlie still thought she wouldn't remember him fondly unless he performed some great feat.

Yes, that was very sad.

She had always felt a special closeness to that old man. But obviously, she had not conveyed it well.

As she brushed the animal with wider and wider strokes, she began to feel that something was unfinished, that she had to do something else.

And a strange thought kept rising in her mind—that she wanted to avenge the horrific assault on Charlie, the steel shot ripping and tearing through his innards.

It was a stupid thought. Vengeance for what? Who? Why?

But it was there.

As she was mulling over this vengeance, she realized she still had not turned the check Rose had sent her over to Mikoyan or Allie.

She had not even mentioned the $22,000.

Didi finished her grooming of the horse, gave him a succulent carrot, and walked outside. Huck, the Corgi, was fast asleep in the doorway and she had to step over him to exit.

The day was absolutely beautiful. Everything was tranquil. Why were her thoughts so violent? Vengeance? She was a healer.

What kind of vengeance do you extract from the world when the man whose wounds you are avenging is eighty years old and seemed willing to leap happily into the grave? And when the individuals who assaulted him were either dead or in jail? And when the one who had paid for the attack was going away for a long prison term?

A swatch of color suddenly caught Didi's eye. She saw Mrs. Tunney cleaning the kitchen mats in the yard behind the house, right over the spot where Didi usually did her morning yoga.

Didi grinned.

She remembered what her mother used to say: "The best vengeance for Christians is to give the people you hate the most what they want the most."

Had she been talking about sex? Pastries? Money?

Didi never knew.

The thought came to her that the person she hated most right now was herself.

And what did Didi Nightingale want most?

She reflected.

It would have to be, she realized, to wake up in the morning, go outside to do her yoga, and see a herd of dairy cows grazing in her fields.

She burst out laughing and then did a wild pirouette, falling down in the process.

Seated on the ground, she wondered how many dairy cows and milking machines $22,000 could buy. Probably a respectable number of both at the current, depressed prices. And she would call it . . . the herd that Charlie built.

No! No! The herd that Charlie *and* Rose built.

She stood up and slapped at her jeans to get the dirt off. *I am acting like a child*, she thought.

Didi headed toward the house.

Halfway there, she stopped and thought: *No! I am not acting like a child. I am acting like an idiot!*

Buy cows with Rose's money?

She knew now where Rose's money had come from—extortion. It was dirty money. It didn't matter that Rose had been extorting money from a criminal. It didn't matter that her motives might have been good. The money was dirty, tainted, and lousy with death.

And even if it had been the cleanest money in the world, the last thing Didi needed was a cash-draining cow herd. Veterinarians were supposed to treat cows, not milk them.

She continued her journey back to the house, walking faster, making a no-nonsense mental list of things she had to do immediately.

One. Send Rose's check to Mikoyan.

Two. Buy Allie Voegler a good dinner with a third party present to avoid either a fight or a reconciliation.

Three. Give Mrs. Tunney some cash to buy flowers for Charlie.

Four. Apply for a bank loan to expand her small animal practice.

Five. Visit that dream lady—Lily.

She opened the door, stopped in her tracks, and angrily scratched Number Five from her list.

Why would she want to visit the dream lady? No dreams were obsessing her. And, even if one was, she wanted no part of dream interpretations involving violent demises and fond remembrances.

Quickly, she substituted a new Number Five—give Rose's dog, Huck, a bath.

Charlie Gravis regained consciousness seventy-seven hours after he was hospitalized.

He looked around, confused. All he could see at first was the color green. It took him a while to realize he was in a bed in a room with light green walls and ceiling.

Then he saw other beds in the room and people in those beds attached to machines. He realized that he, too, was attached.

It didn't bother him in the least. He fell asleep.

He woke an hour later. Two women were fiddling with his body. They wore white. The revelation came—he was in the hospital.

That was strange. He felt so good, so calm, so . . . well, yes . . . happy. There was a funny, continuous fluttering in his stomach, as if someone was in there poking around with a velvet shovel. But it wasn't at all unpleasant.

One of the women put her face right next to his and asked: "How do you feel, Mr. Gravis?"

Charlie didn't know what to say. He just smiled. She patted his arm and said: "You'll be out of intensive care in the morning."

He fell asleep and woke again. It must be night now, he realized. Every sound was muted.

Now his stomach didn't feel so good. In fact, it hurt and he was a bit nauseous.

But for the first time since he had first regained consciousness, he remembered why he was there.

It was the strangest thing. Harland Frick had shot him.

Charlie remembered walking toward Harland with his ax—but once he realized it was Harland he certainly wasn't going to do any harm with it.

And then *boom*! Just like that! Old Harland had pulled the trigger.

Remembering clearly now, Charlie was very confused.

He and Ike had been waiting in the barn for Burt Conyers. They had set the trap for the poet because he had murdered Rose Vigdor.

Why had Harland and his assistant shown up? It didn't make no sense at all.

Charlie lay there, thinking, brooding, watching the lights of the monitoring machines flicker in the gloom.

His mind was becoming more and more insightful, he realized. His synapses were beginning to fire.

And then it came to him—with such force that he tried to sit up. That was a mistake. He flopped back down. The pain was becoming intense, but that didn't matter.

He had the solution to the mystery. He knew why Harland had come to the barn!

To steal his manuscript!

It was clear that Harland had hustled him from the beginning. Harland had told him that "Cows and Me" was essentially a children's book. This was part of the hustle—to discourage Charlie. To make him give up the project.

Why?

Charlie grinned through his pain.

That sly old fox had known early on that "Cows and Me" was a multimillion-dollar project—potentially.

Harland knew that the finished book would be so powerful there would be movies and TV dramas spun off—with Jon Voight playing the Charlie Gravis part, the wise old dairy farmer.

Poor Harland. He had gambled all and lost.

Only he, Charlie, was left standing, with all the marbles.

A lady came in with some pills. She said: "My, you look happy, Mr. Gravis."

Charlie winked at her and swallowed the pills.

As he began to drift off to sleep, he started planning what he would do with the money once he finished the manuscript.

One thing was sure. He wouldn't leave Doc Nightingale high and dry without a veterinary assistant.

When the money started pouring in, he would give her at least three weeks' notice.

Signet

Selma Eichler

"A highly entertaining series"
—Carolyn Hart

"Finally there's a private eye we can embrace..." *—Joan Hess*

☐ MURDER CAN SPOOK YOUR CAT	0-451-19217-6/$5.99
☐ MURDER CAN WRECK YOUR REUNION	0-451-18521-8/$5.99
☐ MURDER CAN STUNT YOUR GROWTH	0-451-18514-5/$5.99
☐ MURDER CAN KILL YOUR SOCIAL LIFE	0-451-18139-5/$5.99
☐ MURDER CAN SPOIL YOUR APPETITE	0-451-19958-8/$5.99
☐ MURDER CAN UPSET YOUR MOTHER	0-451-20251-1/$5.99